Basic Instincts

NOTHING BUT THE NIGHT

THOM COLLINS

ENTWINED PUBLISHING

NOTHING BUT THE NIGHT

Chapter One

A Potential Scandal

The luxury of a good night's sleep was something Marc Glass had learnt to live without. For several years he'd been getting by on three to four hours. Five was a rare indulgence. He couldn't bear to lie in bed, idly staring into the dark, knowing there was no chance of falling off again. As soon as his eyes opened, he was wide awake. Two years earlier he had taken up late-night running, in the hope that physical exhaustion would be the trigger he needed for a full night of rest. While it helped him to fall asleep quickly, he still found himself alert at four a.m. most mornings.

Usually, he would get straight up and begin work, but some days, like this one, he pulled on his running shoes and went for another pre-dawn run.

It had gone six-thirty as he pounded the coastal path on the return route to the house. He had been out for an hour. The darkness and cold of a wet March morning did not deter him. He didn't feel the cold or the drizzle when he was running. A podcast on Blyham history in the eighteenth century had occupied his mind for most of the course. Now that it had finished, his mind turned to the day ahead.

There was a sliver of light grey sky on the horizon. Sunrise was about half an hour away. The forecast was for cloud and rain for the rest of the week. Typical Blyham weather for this time of year. Not that it mattered. Marc had a full day of meetings planned, both at the factory and online with overseas buyers. There was a good chance he wouldn't breathe fresh air again until his night-time run that evening, and he was already looking forward to the next episode of the podcast.

Through the week, one day was much like another. A cycle of exercise and work peppered with a couple of visits to his parents. They would cook dinner for him one evening and he would take then out for a meal on the other. Tonight, he had to fend for himself. He'd stay late at the factory to delay his return to an empty house. Probably pick up some food on his way home. Nothing too heavy. Not when he'd have to run it off later.

The drizzle strengthened into rain. Marc swiped his arm across his face, wiping the sweat and water away.

He still had his ear-pods in, but could hear the violent crash of waves below, battering the rocky outcrop beneath the cliffs. It sounded like things were getting rougher than had been forecast. If a storm was coming in, he'd just have to complete his evening exercises in his home gym, though he preferred the freshness and exposure of a night run.

Almost home, he put on an extra burst of speed for the last mile, coming off the track and onto the main road that led to the house. His breath rasped, searing his lungs and throat, pain burning in his thighs and calf muscles, but he powered through. Pain was good. Pain was a real sensation. It meant he was still alive.

As he turned onto the drive he saw a strange car parked in front of the garage. A dark BMW.

Marc slowed to a stop. His breath grated in his ears, and he removed the pods. He sucked in a chest full of air through his mouth. His heart pounded.

The driver's door of the car opened, and an umbrella poked out and was put up. A woman with blonde hair stepped from the car. She was petite, in a pale trouser suit and impractical high heels. Marc rubbed his eyes and blinked away the stinging sweat, trying to focus. There was something familiar about the woman.

She approached with a tight, humourless smile. Beneath the umbrella, her hair was a blow-dried miracle. She must have got up as early as he had to achieve that look.

"I'd heard you were an early riser," she said. Elocution and speech training couldn't mask the original Geordie tones in her accent. "I thought I had already missed you. Ten more minutes and I was going to head over to the factory."

Marc froze as he realised just who his visitor was.

Nadine Smythe.

He stepped around her, heading for the house. "You wasted your time coming here."

The rain turned into a downpour. He took shelter beneath the front porch. He left the key under a rock in the garden when he went running, but he didn't want to retrieve it in front of Nadine. She would think nothing of letting herself in another time.

"I've come about your brother," she said, stepping onto the porch. She put down the umbrella and shook it out. "Awful morning, isn't it? I should have brought a raincoat but it was dry when I left home."

"You shouldn't be here at all. I've got nothing to say to you."

"Don't be like that. You should be pleased someone cares enough about Theo to follow up the story."

"My brother is not a story," he snapped.

Nadine Smythe was a journalist for *The Blyham Chronicle*. She also had her own podcast where she *"exposed injustices and laid bare the truth."* She was beginning to gain fame beyond local news and had appeared on several national breakfast and mid-morning TV shows offering her opinions on news and current events. Her opinions were always bombastically right wing.

"You're wrong there," she said, her cold stare boring into him. "I've been working on this for several weeks and there's most definitely a story. And I'm going to tell it. I'm giving you the opportunity to be part of it. To put your family's position across."

"I think you've done enough damage to me and my family already. The answer is no. Now get back in your car and take it off my drive."

"I think Theo was murdered." She let the words drop like bombs, studying his face for a reaction.

Marc had learnt the hard way to keep his emotions to himself. He would never allow a hack like Nadine to read him.

His face was stone.

Inside he was a mess.

She had given voice to the words he had only dared to think.

"He's been dead three months," he managed to say. "Why your sudden interest?"

Nadine edged closer. "There's nothing sudden about it. I was researching a story that involved Theo before he died. When his death appeared to be an accident, I thought I had lost my lead. I was wrong."

"What are talking about?" Marc made no effort to hide the contempt in his voice. As well as stoking the rage of the Alt-right, Nadine's podcast was big on conspiracy theories. He doubted she believed most of the shit she shared, but she wouldn't let something as trivial as her personal beliefs get in the way of her rising profile.

"Your brother was involved with some important people. You know that much, right? He was a sex worker. A popular one, by all accounts."

And there it was. The true reason for her interest. A salacious sex scandal. A *gay* sex scandal at that. He could already hear the indignant tone of her broadcast. The moral outrage her reports would stir up. "Leave," he snapped, jabbing his finger towards the road.

"Theo was killed because of what he knew. Because of *whom* he knew. I know you don't like me, Marc, but you must care about seeing justice done. For the sake of your little brother. C'mon, surely you can put our differences aside to get to the truth."

"Theo was killed in a hit-and-run. It was an accident."

"And the driver has never been traced. The car was stolen and burnt without a scrap of evidence remaining. I don't believe you're satisfied with that conclusion. Not when your brother was providing sexual services to a Tory back-bencher."

He raised his hand. "Enough…" Anxiety wrapped its suffocating tendrils around his chest. His breath was fast and shallow. He closed his eyes and fought against it, disgusted with himself for allowing her to see that she had got to him.

"I'm not looking to trash Theo's memory. I promise that. Theo was a small part of a bigger story. An important part. I believe he lost his life because of it. We can put that right and expose the people behind it."

Theo Glass had been no saint. Marc was aware of that. He didn't know the details of everything his brother had been involved in, but he knew enough. Theo had taken delight in shocking him, bragging about his online content. About how many followers he had on social media, how many paid subscribers there were for his sexual site. Marc had seen how far Theo went with the images and videos he posted on his open X profile. He didn't want to know what he was doing behind the paywall of Hot-4-Fans and other subscription sites. There was escorting too. Like a lot of younger people, Theo believed he was from the first generation to embrace sex and pleasure. He thought he could provoke his older brother with the details of his life. Theo hadn't realised that Marc wasn't shocked. The truth was he just wasn't interested. He had bigger problems than worrying about his brother selling his arse to wealthy older men. All that mattered was that Theo didn't tell their parents what he was doing.

If Nadine went ahead with this muck-raking article, there would no way of keeping it from them. They had a copy of *The Blyham Chronicle* delivered each morning. Their hearts hadn't recovered from the death of their youngest son. The shock of how he'd earnt a living might finish them off.

"Please, Nadine, don't do this. The police are still investigating his death. Leave it to them."

"Blyham police," she sneered. "They don't give a shit. The case remains open in name only. There's not a single officer actively investigating. C'mon, wake up. Your brother was fucking the Member of Parliament for Blyham South. The pressure from above to make this disappear is immense."

"You know that for a fact?"

"Of course I fucking do. I've got contacts in the force who have told me exactly that."

"On the record?"

She rolled her eyes. "What do you think? They want to keep their jobs."

"Then you've got nothing. This is more of your conspiracy bullshit. It plays well on those crappy news channels you go on, but it's not reality. Now go, before I call the police to move you on. And if you doorstep me like this again, I'll phone your editor and report you for harassment."

Nadine accepted defeat and put up her umbrella. "This isn't harassment, it's journalism. Whether you like it or not, your brother's death is part of a story and I'm going to write it. If you want to do justice to his memory, you know where to find me."

Marc stood on the porch and watched her walk back to the car. He waited until she was inside and had started the engine. The rain bounced six inches off the roof as she reversed into a U-turn and drove away. The sky had lightened to a miserable shade of grey.

Fuck.

He'd known when he'd woken up at four this morning that this was going to be a shitty day and his instinct had been correct.

Marc retrieved the hidden key and went into the house. He kicked off his muddy running shoes at the front door and strode to the kitchen in his socks. His mind galloped ahead, so much information rushing through his brain. He'd had dealings with Nadine Smythe before. She was dangerous, borderline psychopathic in his opinion, but she was determined. She thought she was on to a big story and that was it. She wouldn't let it go. The sensational detail of his brother's life prior to his death would be exposed and scandalised in her shitty newspaper and podcast. He could already see her sitting on a breakfast TV sofa, smug in her moral superiority, delighting in the shock she caused, oblivious to the devastation her story would bring.

Marc couldn't allow it. His parents had suffered enough. Theo had died in early December. Marc had thought their first Christmas without him was going to break them, but they'd got through it. Their grief was tottering on the edge of the acceptance stage.

Nadine Smythe would set them right back.

Unless he did something about it.

Chapter Two

The Detective

By the following afternoon, the rain had still not stopped. When Marc drove into the centre of Blyham at five p.m. it had got considerably worse. He parked in a multi-storey and hurried towards Upper Salvin Road. The rain came at him in horizontal strokes. It sloshed around his feet and when he reached his destination, he was soaked through. His trousers clung to his legs and the wetness went right through to his underpants.

He had never noticed the doorway to the Blair and Co Detective Agency before, even though he'd used both the newsagents and the coffee shop that stood on either side of it. A dark-green door led into a small, gloomy hallway. There was nowhere to go but straight up the stairs. He reached a landing with four glass-panelled doors leading off from it. The first door was marked with a sign reading 'Reception', so he went in there.

It was an old-fashioned room with blown vinyl wallpaper that looked like it had been painted over countless times. There were green carpet tiles on the floor and four high-backed chairs lined up beneath the window. Marc realised he was dripping, pulled a handkerchief from his inner pocket — that was thankfully dry — and wiped his face and neck.

A slim woman in her mid-twenties with long auburn hair tied in a ponytail sat at the small desk in a room that had little natural light.

"Isn't it awful?" she said, taking in Marc's soaking state. "If you go back into the hall and take the first door at the top of the stairs, there are paper towels in the bathroom. You might be able to soak up the worst of it."

"Thank you. It's Marc Glass. I have an appointment with er…Jason Durham."

The girl consulted an old-fashioned desk diary and nodded. Her name badge read Olivia. "Go and get yourself dry and I'll let Jason know you're here."

He thanked her again and followed her directions. Like the rest of the office, the bathroom was outdated. It would have benefitted from a redesign twenty years ago, but it was clean and there was an abundance of paper towels. Marc patted his hair dry and wiped the worst of the wetness from his trousers. It would have to do. He knew he wouldn't fully dry until he got home and stripped these wet things off.

"Just go straight through," Olivia told him on his return. "He's expecting you. I'll bring you a drink to warm you up. What would you like? Cappuccino? Latte? I've got a machine that does them all."

"A tea would be great," he said. "Just a splash of milk. No sugar."

Olivia gave him a winning smile and said she'd bring it in shortly. Marc took an instant liking to her. As a businessman, he knew the crucial importance of having a great person on the front door to make clients feel welcomed and valued. While the initial appearance of Blair and Co was not encouraging, in a couple of minutes Olivia had turned his attitude around.

This might not turn out to be a complete waste of time after all.

A man in his early thirties stood in the doorway of the office at the farthest end of the gloomy hall. He was little more than a silhouette lit from behind. Marc could see he was dressed in navy chinos, black brogues and an open-necked blue shirt.

"Mr Glass," he said. "I'm Jason, come on in."

He was a couple of inches shorter than Marc, but well built. He wore a heady-smelling aftershave that failed to hide the notes of alcohol on his breath as they passed.

"Thanks for coming in," Jason said. "I've already had two cancellations this afternoon due to the weather." He gestured for Marc to take a seat and walked around the other side of the desk.

Marc saw him fully for the first time and was startled. At forty-four, it had been a long time since he'd been instantly affected by the physical appearance of a man, but Jason was stunning. It was his large, expressive eyes that first drew him in. They were a pale shade, somewhere between green and blue, and they gave a boyish quality to his masculine face. His dark-blond hair was swept to the right, short at the back and sides with a little length on top. He had a well-trimmed beard, brown and seasoned with flecks of grey. His mouth was wide. Marc had the most insane urge to kiss it. When he smiled, he revealed a small gap between his two front teeth, which only made him even sexier.

The body beneath his clothes was fit. More athletic than muscled, and there was an almost military bearing about his posture, with his shoulders back and his chest held proudly.

Jason sat and leaned across the file on his desk, looking at the notes, granting Marc a peek down the open neck of his shirt, and a tantalising hint of chest hair.

Get hold of yourself. Remember the reason you are here.

"So, this is about your brother?" Jason said, reading the file. Marc had given the briefest summary of his case to Olivia when he'd called to make the appointment yesterday.

"Yes, but it's probably not what you're thinking. My brother isn't missing or anything like what you're used to dealing with."

Jason looked at him with wide, reassuring eyes. "There's no such thing as a usual case in this business. Why don't you start at the beginning and tell me what the problem is."

Marc sighed. The beginning. He didn't even know where that was. "Theo died in December. Down on the waterfront by the Vermont Hotel? You probably heard about it. He was killed by a car as he crossed the road in front of the hotel. Some of the witnesses say the car drove straight at him, but the police were never convinced."

Jason pushed the file to one side. "I'm so sorry to hear that. Yes, I remember it. There must have been CCTV coverage. There are cameras all along the waterfront. And at the hotel too."

"There are, but it's inconclusive whether the car changed course to hit him or not. The resolution of the images isn't great. I must have watched it a million times and even I can't decide on what I'm seeing."

"I take it the driver was never caught. Do you want me to investigate further? See if I can track them down?"

Marc shook his head. "That's not why I'm here. It's more...complicated than that. The car was discovered burned out a few miles away. It was stolen and they never found the driver. Have you heard of Nadine Smythe? The journalist."

Was that a tiny twitch at the corner of Jason's mouth?

Jason nodded. "Of course. Blyham's finest." There was no mistaking the sarcasm in his tone.

"She came to visit me yesterday. She's conducting her own investigation into Theo's death... Theo's murder."

They were interrupted by a knock on the door. Olivia came in bearing two mugs. "Tea, as promised," she said putting a mug in front of Marc. She carried the other around the desk and gave it to Jason. The tea was steaming. Strong and hot, exactly how Marc liked it.

"I'll be getting off now," she said to Jason. "Mr Blair is still with his last client."

"That's fine, Olivia, thanks. Just drop the latch on the front door as you go out. See you tomorrow."

"Have a good night," she said cheerfully. "Goodbye, Mr Glass."

They were alone again.

Jason sat back in his chair. "So, Nadine Smythe. I take it she didn't bring you news on the identity of the hit-and-run driver. She thinks she's got a bigger story?"

Marc nodded grimly. This was easier than he'd expected. Jason had a calm, comfortable manner that diminished his anxiety.

"My brother was always a wild one. I was sixteen when he was born, so we were never as close as most brothers who grow up together. I went to university when he was two years old. We have a sister, Eva. She's three years younger than I am. When Theo came along, he was spoilt. Especially by my mother. She let him get away with things me and Eva would never have been allowed to."

"It's not unusual," Jason said. "Especially with such a large gap between kids. Did Theo get in trouble with the law?"

Marc shook his head. "Not that I'm aware. He could have had a record of petty offences. He'd didn't always think about the consequences before acting out, but it would only have been minor stuff, I'm sure of it. If there was anything at all, I haven't found out about it."

Jason took a sip of tea and waited for him to continue.

"It pains me to speak ill of him, especially now he's not here, but Theo was a brat. As he got older, teenage years and beyond, he was an antagonistic little shit. He did terribly at school. He scraped through his A-levels after two years of hard partying. He didn't think he needed the qualifications because he wanted to be a celebrity. He thought reality TV would be his route to success. If you can think of a show, he applied to be on it. *Big Brother*, *The Voice*, *First Dates*, *Gogglebox*. It didn't go anywhere. He got a job in telesales while he tried to make a name as a vlogger and social media influencer. Again, with little to no success."

"Okay. Why is Nadine so interested in Theo? It doesn't sound like her kind of story at all."

Marc took a sip of his own tea. "Have you heard of websites like Hot-4-Fans and Only Fans?"

"Yes."

"That's where Theo found his level. Customers paid to watch videos of him. I never saw any of what he was up to myself, but he got a kick out of telling me about it. I think he thought it would shock me. I questioned a couple of his friends after the funeral. They were pretty tight-lipped, but I understand it started off in a low-key way. Selling nude pictures and videos. That progressed to jerk-off videos and then using toys and soon enough he was making adult content with other models."

"It's not illegal," Jason said, matter-of-factly. "It's not even that remarkable. Lots of people turned to online sex work during the pandemic. It isn't a big deal. If Nadine thinks she can slut-shame the victim of a hit-and-run over some sex tapes she might find, she's on the wrong side of cancel culture." His eyes were like deep, beautiful pools. Marc could easily get lost in them. Gorgeous men could sometimes make him nervous, but not Jason. His good looks somehow made him more reassuring and trustworthy.

Marc swallowed. "That's still not the story. I'm just filling you in on my brother's lifestyle. He said he was proud of it, though he never told our parents. He told me he made a fortune. Theo was prone to exaggeration, but he did have more cash to play with in the couple of years before his death. It's possible he made a decent living with the online gigs, supplemented with escort work."

"Escorting?"

They had reached the heart of the matter. The fact of Theo's life that Nadine was really interested in.

"My brother told me at a family barbecue last summer that he had a high-profile client. Well, no, he didn't just tell me, he bragged about it." Marc exhaled. The story was becoming harder to tell. He'd only come to realise in the weeks since Theo's death that his brother had suffered from serious self-esteem problems. He'd genuinely believed that fucking famous people made him important too. "I told him I didn't want to know, but by the end of the day, after a lot of drinks, he couldn't stop himself. He was desperate to tell me. Whether it was to shock or impress, I'll never know."

Jason's brow rose with the question. "Can you tell me who it was?"

Marc unconsciously glanced over his shoulder, determining that they were alone, that they couldn't be overheard. Despite that, he lowered his voice. "Soloman Archer."

At first, Jason didn't react, then, as the name made sense to him, he let out a low whistle. "Shit. Now that would be a story for the press."

Soloman Archer was the MP for Blyham South and, though he was just a back-bencher in Parliament, he was seen as one to watch for the future. His ambition and hunger for a top job in government were on public record. A stocky, blue-eyed silver fox and, in Marc's opinion, a smooth-talking liar. He'd scraped through the last general election when the Labour and Liberal Democrat vote was split in Blyham, allowing the Tories to slither through the crack. Soloman lived with his wife and kids in Wiltshire, about as far from Blyham as it was possible to get, but he'd still managed to make a name for himself in the local area. He'd become an even bigger name if Nadine Smythe got her way.

"So Soloman is what...? About twenty years older than Theo?"

Marc nodded. "At least. And married."

"Nadine's interest is beginning to make sense," Jason said.

Marc spread his hands on the table. "It's not just a sex scandal, MP uses sex workers on the side. Where's the mileage in that? It's almost like a rite of passage for that lot. When she doorstepped me yesterday, Nadine alluded to Soloman having something to do with Theo's death. That the circumstances were suspicious."

"You don't think so?"

"Not as such. I know it's the stuff of conspiracy thrillers, but it's unlikely there's anything in it. Soloman has a lot to lose, after all. It's just... Oh, I don't know." He glanced out of the window. The rain continued to come down in blinding sheets. He'd get soaked again going back to the car.

"If Nadine thinks there's something in the theory, she's going to pursue, and if she finds the evidence, she'll expose it. I have no doubt about it." Jason's voice was kind. His expression sympathetic. "What I'm trying to say is—what do you want me to do? I won't be able to kill the story if she finds the evidence she needs."

Marc took another sip of tea. His mouth was exceptionally dry. "I know. I've already told you Theo was my mother's golden boy. It will destroy her if just a tiny bit of the story turns out to be true. I want you to investigate Theo's life too. Find out exactly what he was up to in the months before he died. Who he was involved with. If there's any truth to the escorting claims and whether he was really involved with Soloman, or if it was just an attention-seeking lie. I'd rather my parents heard the truth from me than read about it in the papers first. I would do it myself, but I don't want to go through all those movies he made. It's one thing to hear about it, it's something else to watch your brother getting his brains banged out for some sad form of validation."

Jason didn't speak for a moment. He studied Marc carefully across the desk. Finally, he said, "You might not like what I discover."

Marc let out a bitter laugh. "I know I'm not going to like it. I don't like anything about it. But it's the only thing I can do right now to protect my family. Knowledge is power, right?"

Jason didn't answer. He kept looking at Marc while the rain raked against the window.

Chapter Three

An Unusual Case

"I don't know what to make of it." Jason Durham drained the pint glass of beer to the bottom. "I'll go to the bar and get us another. You can tell me what you think when I come back."

"Just a Coke for me," said Ryman Blair, his business partner. "I've got to drive home after this. I need to pick Chloe up from swimming in" — he checked his watch — "forty minutes."

Jason slid out of his chair and crossed the wood-panelled room to the bar. The torrential rain had not stopped, and the wooden floor was starting to take on the heady smell of damp. His trousers were still wet around the calves. The New Inn was a three-minute walk from the office, but Jason and Ryman had got soaked as they pelted down the street.

It had just gone six-thirty. Most evenings at this time the pub would be doing a decent post-work trade, but the filthy weather had kept a lot of punters away. There were only three other customers in the bar. Jason ordered another pint of craft ale for himself and the

Coke for Ryman then carried the drinks back to the table.

Though they were just a two-man detective agency, Ryman was the founder of the business and the senior partner. He was forty-six, built like a mountain, and Jason's best friend as well as colleague.

"Well?" Jason asked, slipping into the seat. His trousers were damp on the arse too and he shuffled to get comfortable.

"I don't see what the problem is," Ryman said, shrugging his shoulders. "It sounds interesting to me."

"But Soloman Archer. I don't know. A man like that could close us down if he catches me snooping into his private life. He's connected."

"Fuck him." Ryman laughed. "Seriously? You can't be scared of him? He'll be out at the next election. Maybe well before that if Nadine's story has any truth to it. The man's on borrowed time."

"It's not just that. The whole sex angle makes me feel awkward. Do I really want to trawl through the sexual activities of a dead man?"

There was something about the whole case that made Jason uneasy. He couldn't nail it down to anything more than a niggling feeling, but it wouldn't go away.

"You'll be helping a grieving family. Nadine's suspicions about Soloman are probably nothing more than bullshit, but if she thinks she's got enough juice on Theo, she'll run with that instead. You might be able to head her off and bury the details before she can even find them."

"Hmm." Jason sipped the foamy head off his pint.

"It's not like you to be prudish."

"I'm not."

"So why are you clutching your pearls because the victim was a sex worker. He deserves justice as much as any client. Take the bloody case."

Jason sighed. Ryman was right, as always. "I don't know what's wrong with me. It's strange, that's all. Why doesn't this Marc guy just tell his parents anyway? Why does he want all this evidence."

"Didn't he say Theo was the parents' favourite? They won't believe a word Marc says against him unless he's got solid proof. They're as likely to turn on him for tarnishing the memory of their precious child."

Jason had already done a quick search on Theo Glass, or rather Hart Stone as he was known online. It hadn't taken long to find his Hot-4-Fans profile, and while the sexy stuff was hidden behind a paywall, Theo had posted plenty of explicit photos and videos to his free social media accounts to drum up business. It was all there, if you knew where to look. He was a good-looking lad who'd managed to hang on to his twinky appeal well into his late twenties. He had a lot of followers too, even now. The connection between Theo Glass, the Blyham man killed in a hit-and-run, and Hart Stone, the self-described hot-to-fuck-cum-dump, hadn't been made. There was no mention on any of the Hart Stone accounts that he had died.

Jason took a long swallow. The ale was going someway towards easing his tension.

"Maybe you're right," he said. "If Marc wants to pay us to dig around his brother's personal life, we shouldn't complain."

"Exactly. It sounds like an easy job."

"Have you heard of Marc Glass?" Jason asked.

Ryman furrowed his brow. "Should I have?"

Jason pulled out his phone and tapped the screen. "I did a quick internet search on him too. It turns out he's kind of famous. You know the TV show *The Partnership*? He was on that. It was a few years ago now, but he actually won it."

The Partnership was a blatant rip-off of *The Apprentice*, a reality TV show in which fifteen hopefuls competed against each other in business-themed challenges. One contestant was eliminated after each episode with the ultimate winner taking home a £200,000 investment. Marc had used the prize money to set up a factory in Peterlee that produced farming machinery. In the few minutes Jason had spent snooping, the business seemed like a big deal, exporting products worldwide.

He brought up a photo of Marc from when he was on the show. He was a lot younger-looking. It was a good fifteen years since his win.

Ryman looked at the phone. "Oh, yeah. I do remember him. I never watched it, but it was everywhere at the time. He was in the local papers and news stations. They loved that Blyham-boy-made-good story. He's done well for himself."

"Another reason for Nadine Smythe to be interested in the story, don't you think? An MP, a dead sex worker and the reality TV star brother."

"It ticks a lot of boxes. And another reason to beat her to the punch, don't you think?"

"Go on then, you've got me. I'll take the case."

"We can't afford for you not to," Ryman said.

"Things aren't that bad."

"There're not that great, either. We need every decent job we can get. Besides, this one will be a walk in the park for you. I don't know what you're worried about."

When Ryman left to collect his daughter, Jason considered staying for another drink, but the atmosphere in The New Inn was nonexistent. The weather was no better, and it was clear that most people had decided to stay home. He'd walked to work that morning and with no desire to get soaked again walking back, he arranged an Uber.

Home was a rented two-bedroom flat in a modern building overlooking the river Bly. The rent was extortionate, but he loved living in the heart of the city too much to find somewhere cheaper. The dash from the car to the foyer meant he was soaked all the way through again.

Jason poured a strong vodka and Coke and turned on the air-fryer before going to the bedroom. He stripped naked and took a quick shower to warm his cold skin. Freshly dried, he pulled on an old T-shirt and a pair of pyjama bottoms. He was thinking about Marc again when he put a chicken breast on to cook and mixed up some couscous with chopped peppers.

The one thing he hadn't admitted to Ryman was just how attractive he found his new client. He'd have to be blind not to. Marc was hot. *Incredibly*. He was tall and athletically built with grey-blue eyes and a rugged, square jaw. His beard and short brown hair were streaked with grey, which only made him more attractive. He was quite serious-looking, and sexy rather than traditionally handsome. Some people might not find him attractive at all, but to Jason's eyes he was a near ten out of ten.

Which was another thing that made him uncomfortable.

From a professional angle, it was much better not to fancy the client.

While Marc had talked him through the details of the case, Jason had had to force himself to focus. To stop wondering what he looked like naked, and how big his dick was. While the investigation would involve him looking over the many hours of sex tape footage shot by his brother, all Jason wanted to do was look at naked photos of Marc. Or, even better, the real thing.

Get a grip. You work for the man now. You can't think like this.

Jason plated up his dinner and ate it at the kitchen counter with a twenty-four-hour news channel playing on the TV in the background. He didn't pay much attention to the headlines — his mind was already elsewhere, still thinking about Marc and the case. Once he'd finished and loaded the dishwasher, he poured another vodka and retired to the sofa with his laptop and notebook. He knew he should begin with a deep dive into Theo Glass, but when he opened a search tab, it was Marc's name he entered.

The hits all related to his success on *The Partnership*, accompanied with lots of photos of the fresh-faced winner. Marc had been twenty-nine at the time. He didn't have a beard back then and his hair was all brown. He was square-jawed and good-looking, but lacked the characteristics of the man he had met today. Now in his mid-forties, Marc had certainly improved with age.

After a quick trawl of his Wikipedia bio, Jason discovered that Marc had been married, and his husband had died in 2021. Another rapid search revealed the reason for Marc's distrust of Nadine Smythe.

The Partnership's star's husband dies of Covid read her headline. The accompanying article was full of hyperbole and inflammatory language, illustrated by photos of an exhausted-looking Marc wearing a face mask to visit the hospital. An even more intrusive shot further down showed Marc crying in his car, gripping the wheel, pain and grief carved across his face.

"You nasty bitch," Jason muttered. *No wonder he hates you.*

There was another photograph of the couple in happier times. Jack Badiel and Marc Glass were a handsome pair. They were around the same age and build. Jack had warm brown eyes and an infectious smile. It was a surprise to see Marc, who had appeared so serious-looking, smiling so widely beside him. Their love for each other was clear in the image. They made a beautiful pair.

Jack's funeral had taken place at the height of the Covid-19 restrictions, when such events had been limited to immediate family only. That hadn't stopped the *Blyham Chronicle* photographer from intruding on their grief. Long-lensed images had captured Marc's anguish as he and four other mourners accompanied Jack's coffin into the crematorium.

Jason found himself simmering in anger on their behalf. The man's misery had already been exploited once for the sake of a splashy headline — now the same shitty journalist and paper wanted to do it all over again. Marc's husband and his brother had died well before their time. What Nadine was doing was all wrong.

Marc had approached the agency seeking help.

Jason was determined to provide it.

He closed the tabs on Marc and opened a new window, this time searching for 'Hart Stone Hot-4-Fans'. Nadine would base her story around Theo's sex work, so that's where he'd have to start. He soon discovered that Hart Stone had profiles on more than one adult platform. It was distasteful that they were all still open to new subscribers. He guessed that Marc had limited knowledge of how these websites worked and probably didn't know where to begin to get them closed down. Jason made a note to start the process in the morning, but, for now, he needed access.

He took out subscriptions on each of the sites and began to work through them, video by video. The bulk of Theo's content was solo stuff—wanking, showing off, playing with a variety of dildos. He wasn't interested in any of those just yet, and instead focused on the clips where he appeared with other performers.

The first was titled *Cummer X ruins my tight boy hole*. Jason clicked on the video and began to take notes. Cummer X was a muscular black man with an enormous cock. They were obviously in a hotel room. Jason paused the clip to study the room, searching for any small details that might give away where they were. They'd been smart enough to remove the bed runners and pillows bearing any motif. They had also cleared the dresser of room service menus and tourist information. From the size of the room, and the quality of the bedding and décor, this was no cheap motel. Jason scribbled a note—*hotel 4 stars and above?*

He restarted the clip and concentrated on what he could hear.

Theo's dialogue was cringy. "Destroy this white boy pussy with your big black cock." Despite the bad porn histrionics, his northern accent came through clearly.

Cummer X bent the white boy over the dresser and pounded his arse mercilessly.

"Take this big black cock," Cummer said. His delivery was as stiff as his dick, but Jason noted another northeast accent. If they were both local boys, then it was highly likely they had shot this in one of the nearby hotels. The Vermont? Theo had been close to there when he was hit by the car that had killed him. He scribbled more notes.

The camera swept between Cummer's legs to get a clear shot of his cock sliding in and out of Theo and his balls slapping his underside with each inward thrust. That meant they hadn't filmed themselves with cameras on tripods. There was at least one other person in the room with them.

Jason updated his notes and got up to make another vodka and Coke. He had a massive task ahead. He'd have to go through each of these collaborations and find out how many other performers Theo regularly worked with, then it would be a process of cross-referencing with their accounts and social media profiles to see if he could contact any of them.

If he could speak to Cummer X or any of the other models, he'd gain valuable insight into Theo's life. The more he discovered, the more he'd be able to help Marc.

It was going to be a long night with no guarantee that he would find anything, but Jason would not be deterred. He hit play on the next clip.

Chapter Four

Hostile Reception

Jason was surprised to check his messages the following morning and discover that, of the eight men he'd reached out to overnight, two had already replied. Cummer X and a guy who performed under the name of Trace Grey. Trace was one of Theo's more unlikely co-stars. A pale-skinned, thin young man with a sour expression. He would never have troubled the porn world were it not for his massive penis. He boasted in his profile that it was thirteen inches long. Jason didn't doubt it. The beast was out of all proportion with his slight frame. His reply to Jason was to the point:

Get to fuck.

When Jason attempted to communicate further, he found that Trace had blocked him on all of his socials. *Interesting.* He made a note to dig a little deeper into Trace's real identity.

Cummer X was more forthcoming.

Theo was a nice guy. I liked him a lot. I'll help in any way I can.

He even provided Jason with a phone number. *Jackpot.*

Jason quickly keyed the number into his phone and hit dial. After a few rings it went straight to voice mail.

"Hi, this is Dan. Leave a message and I'll call you back."

So, his real name was Dan. This was an encouraging start. Dan was clearly comfortable to share with him and had made no attempt to hide his identity. "Hi, Dan. This is Jason Durham, regarding Theo Glass. I appreciate your willingness to give me your number. Please call me back when you get this message. I'd love to talk to you."

Jason showered, clipped his beard to a tidy stubble and got dressed. He put on one of his favourite jockstraps, a burgundy pouch with a thick, logoed waistband and wide white straps. He usually kept his jocks for weekend wear, but today he felt like wearing something sexier than his basic work briefs. Jockstraps gave him an extra confidence. Made him feel more attractive. He loved the pressure of the straps beneath his bare butt cheeks.

He checked his arse in the mirror. Jason was ex-military and continued to maintain a disciplined fitness regime in civilian life. Sure, there was a bit more meat on his frame now than when he'd been in service, but it suited him. CrossFit sessions kept him in good shape and the extra weight gave him a strong, beefy arse.

"Not bad," he said to his reflection, slapping his cheeks and watching how they jiggled.

Would Marc find that attractive? Is he a big arse man or more interested in dick?

Jason reminded himself that it didn't matter. Marc was a client, not a potential hook-up.

But as he pulled on a pair of black chinos and a light blue shirt, he couldn't help wondering about Marc's physique. Last night he'd seen every inch of his brother's body, but physically Marc and Theo seemed like complete opposites. Theo had been slender and long-limbed. He'd had pale-blond hair, but the freckles on his forehead and shoulders suggested to Jason that he'd really been ginger and had lightened his hair for a more striking effect. Marc was more manly. Broad and thick-set. His old photos showed that Marc had never been a twinky type. When he'd appeared on *The Partnership*, Marc would have been roughly the same age Theo had been when he died, and he'd been far more masculine even then.

He couldn't imagine Marc bending over and spreading his arse cheeks for all comers, the way Theo had done in so many of his videos.

Though Jason wouldn't mind if he did. He'd drop to his knees and stuff his face between those manly cheeks.

Stop it. For fuck's sake.

What the hell had got into him? Maybe it had been staying up late and watching all that adult content that had put sex firmly on his mind this morning.

He had to get over it. He was a professional with a job to do.

Jason had a good breakfast of natural yoghurt, followed by two poached eggs on sourdough, before putting on his shoes and his waterproof jacket. The torrential rain of yesterday had stopped, but the sky over the river was a leaden grey and he was taking no chances after the soaking he'd got last night.

He went to the underground garage to collect his car. Most days he preferred to walk to the office but today he would have to do a bit of travelling around. He drove a three-year-old Nissan Micra. Hardly the sexiest or sportiest of cars, but it was the perfect vehicle for city driving. Some of the car parks in Blyham were ancient, with parking bays far tighter than most modern vehicles could cope with. Jason was confident that he could get his little Micra into the snuggest of spaces. He also hated driving and had little interest in cars or their specifications. Anything larger would be a waste of fuel and money.

Ryman was in the kitchen when he got to the office, just after eight-thirty. Olivia wouldn't be in until nine-fifteen, after the school run.

"Well?" Ryman asked. The kettle was already boiling. He dropped tea bags into two mugs.

Jason fetched the milk from the fridge. "I'm going to run with it. For a few days at least, to see how much I can find."

Ryman nodded, satisfied.

"I've already started." He told him about the inroads he'd made during the night with Dan, aka Cummer X. "I'm hopeful that some of the other men will contact me today. They may not have seen my messages yet."

"What about the one who told you to get fucked?"

Jason chuckled. "I'll find him eventually. It might just take a bit more digging."

"Anything else?"

"I want to locate the places where Theo shot his films. He seemed to use two locations for the majority of them. One is a hotel, pretty ritzy. I'm sure it's somewhere here in the city. The other looks like a private bedroom. I'm wondering whether Theo or one of the other models fitted out one of their own rooms as a private studio and rented it out for filming."

"It's a whole new world," Ryman remarked, pouring boiling water over the tea bags. "I've got a spare room. I wonder if I could spruce it up and earn a bit of extra on the side."

"I doubt you'd get much peace. Those guys seem relentless when it comes to shagging. I don't know how some of them ever walk again after doing the things they do. It goes beyond a full-time job."

"Is it worth it? How much money do they make?"

"I need to speak to Marc about accessing Theo's bank statements, but I can't see how it can be that lucrative. He only charged five pounds for his monthly subscriptions and would often run special officers for as little as three pounds a month. It's less than the price of a cup of coffee. Maybe the online content was only an advertisement for his escorting services. I need to dig further into that."

"And find out whether he really escorted for Soloman Archer."

Jason nodded. "That's the big question, all right."

* * * *

Soloman Archer's constituency office was located in the south side of the city, on a street of terraced houses built in the 1920s. They were all large, three-storey properties that had long since been converted into business space. Soloman was placed between a law firm and a cosmetic surgery clinic.

That afternoon, Jason spent a full fifteen minutes driving around until he found an available parking space, five minutes' walk from the office. He'd spent the bulk of the morning on another case, tracking down a shady accountant in order to serve him with injunction papers. It was drizzling when he got out of the car, and cold, not a damn sight fairer than it had been twenty-four hours earlier. The other cars that lined the streets were all worth three to six times the value of his own humble vehicle.

He rarely had much call to visit this area of the city. It was the moneyed section of Blyham. As he made his way towards Soloman's office, he noted an upmarket hairdresser, an artisan bakery, high-end coffee shops and small boutiques. It was a long way from the chain stores and fast-food eateries of the city centre. These were the kinds of people who would vote for Soloman Archer in an otherwise neglected and deprived city that gained little to no benefit from central government.

Jason had no time for mainstream politics. As far as he was concerned they were all as bent as each other. Come election time, he always voted for the candidate he believed would do the best for the local area, regardless of what party they represented. Soloman Archer would never get his cross on a ballot paper.

He opened the blue front door into a narrow passage. The layout was not dissimilar to the foyer of Blair and Co, only it had been decorated a lot more recently than their own premises had. The carpet, blue of course, still had the smell of newness about it. A large, framed poster of Soloman dominated the wall to the right. *The man who gets things done*, the tagline claimed. He was dressed in a grey suit and navy tie, with his arms folded. There was something almost attractive about his smile, but the humour did not reach his eyes. They gazed blankly at Jason from behind the glass frame.

Is this really the kind of man to fuck cheap male escorts? Soloman didn't seem the type. Jason had spent his lunch break watching a handful of his official videos on YouTube. He was smooth and superficially charming. He talked big about family values and tradition. *Yep, that's exactly the type of hypocrite who resorts to sex workers on the side.*

He went upstairs. The reception area was a lot brighter and more modern than their own office. A woman in her early sixties, with big, wavy hair and large framed glasses, greeted him with a smile.

"Good afternoon. How may I help you?" The words came out without any feeling. A real Stepford receptionist.

"I'd like to speak to Mr Archer."

"Mr Archer is in Parliament at the moment," she had a tone of self-importance.

"And when will he be back on home soil?" Jason gave his most charming smile.

Her eyes wavered uncertainly before she snapped back into efficiency mode. "Mr Soloman's next surgery is a week on Friday. I can check the availability if you'd like to make an appointment."

"Are you in charge around here? When Soloman's away. Miss, er…" He peered at her name badge. "Trish Wait."

"That's Mrs Wait. May I ask what this is about? Mr Archer's time is very limited."

Jason produced his ID. "Jason Durham. I'm a private investigator. Mr Archer is going to want to speak to me sooner rather than later. I can assure you of that, Mrs Wait. Now, when do you think I can talk to him?"

She was thrown. "I...well...I..."

A new voice cut across the room. "What exactly is the problem here?"

An incredibly attractive woman of around fifty had appeared in a doorway to the right. She was tall, with a Pilates-perfect posture and immaculate grooming. Her honey-coloured hair was thick and lush, and her make-up looked like it had been applied by a professional. The creases in her blue trousers were razor sharp, while her cream blouse was made of the highest quality silk. None of that came off a rail.

She spoke to Mrs Wait. "Is there a problem?"

The older woman looked lost. Speech had deserted her.

Jason raised his ID card in the newcomer's direction. "Jason Durham, private investigator. Are you in charge?"

She looked him over with cold eyes. He noticed a slight downward twitch of her mouth. "Chantelle Readymarcher. *Mrs.* I'm Mr Archer's personal assistant."

Of course you are. She looked exactly how he'd imagine a politician's PA would look.

"So, you're the one I need to speak to about arranging a meeting."

Chantelle crossed her arms. "I thought private investigators were supposed to be intelligent. You're either not every bright or you're deaf. Mrs Wait has already explained that you can make an appointment to see Mr Archer at his monthly surgery." She turned to Mrs Wait. "Does Mr Archer have any availability for next week?"

Mrs Wait moved closer to her computer screen and squinted. "It looks like he's fully booked."

Chantelle returned her gaze to Jason, triumph twinkling in her eyes. "There you go then. It will have to be next month. Mrs Wait can book you in for that." She turned dismissively.

"I need to speak to Mr Archer about Theo Glass."

As she turned, he watched her face for any reaction.

She gave an airy shrug. "Am I supposed to know who that is?"

"I don't know," he said, stepping towards her, studying her for any sign that the name registered. "It would depend on how personal your work for Mr Archer goes. You've never heard of Theo?"

Chantelle let out an exasperated sigh and closed her eyes. She opened them again, fixing him with an icy stare. "No. Should I have?"

"Theo Glass was killed by a hit-and-run driver in front of the Vermont Hotel last December."

She softened, just a fraction. "I remember that. It was an accident, as I recall. I don't see what it has to do with Mr Archer."

"It's my understanding that they knew each other."

"And?"

"I need to talk to him about what happened to Theo. And his relationship with him."

Chantelle's mouth took another downward twitch. "And I've already told you, you can make an appointment to see Mr Archer next month. Otherwise, you can direct any questions to him in writing. All of his contact details are available on the website."

"This can't wait."

She didn't flinch. "I'm afraid it will have to. Now, it's time you left."

He would get no further with this one. Chantelle Readymarcher protected her boss like a lioness and her cub. There was one more thing he could try. "If the name Theo Glass doesn't get a reaction from Mr Archer, here's another one you can run by him. Nadine Smythe."

There it was. Almost imperceptible, if he hadn't been looking for it. A slight twitch in the muscles above her mouth. He had struck a nerve.

Jason thrust his card into Chantelle's palm. "Tell your boss that Nadine is researching a story about him and Theo Glass. It's in his best interest to speak to me rather than her."

"Who are you working for? Someone must have hired you."

He'd really caught her now. Jason smiled and moved towards the door. "Just have him call me. He'll be grateful that he did."

Chapter Five

The Co-star

Two days later, Marc contacted Jason for an update on the case. He was in Blyham for a meeting at the conference centre and, when it wrapped up early, he found himself with time to spare.

"Any news?" he asked, surprised by the flighty sensation in his chest at the sound of Jason's voice over the phone.

"Actually, I have made some decent inroads. Are you free to chat?"

"I'm in the city right now. I can drop by the office before I leave." He told Jason where he was.

"I'm in the same area. There's a coffee shop in the foyer of the concert hall, two buildings down from the conference centre."

"I know it." Marc's excitement increased. Why was he so eager to see him again?

"I can meet you there in about fifteen minutes, if that sounds good. I've got things to show you."

Marc asked Jason what he wanted to drink and headed along the waterfront to the concert hall. It was a recent addition to the Blyham riverside development, with impressive mirrored windows from the floor to the roof, reflecting the city during the day, while lighting up from within at night. It was almost directly across the water from the Vermont Hotel, where Theo had taken his final steps.

Marc arrived at the coffee shop in the lull between the daytime trade and the evening crowd who would come out for the shows in another hour. The venue boasted two remarkable halls that catered to all musical tastes, from pop to folk, classical, indie, jazz and opera. He ordered a decaf cappuccino for himself and a large, black Americano for Jason. Then he selected two huge chocolate chip cookies on the side—their denseness looked too good to resist—and found a prime table by the window, with unrestricted views of the river. He'd have to remember this place when he was next in town. It was one of the nicest spots in Blyham and far more relaxed than the chain coffee shops that were on every other street.

A teenaged couple sat at a booth in the corner. They smiled and giggled nervously at each other, clearly on some kind of date. A smart woman sipped black coffee and tapped away at a laptop, while an attractive man in his thirties stared intently at his phone screen. There was a quiet, easy-going vibe about the place that Marc appreciated.

Jason arrived a few minutes later.

Jesus, he's stunning.

He was wearing chinos, an open-necked shirt and a blazer. Marc figured this must be his regular look for work. Smart enough to make a good impression, but not so stuffy that he would alienate the people he needed to talk to.

He wore it well and looked even better than Marc remembered. More handsome, sexier. His eyes were bigger and more expressive. His dark-blond hair was tousled, falling over his brow on the left side. There was a presence about him too, an aura that emanated from within his striking physicality.

"Hi," he said, sliding into the seat opposite. His cologne was fresh and citrusy. No hint of alcohol this time. Marc wondered whether he had imagined it the other day.

"Hi," Marc said, returning Jason's grin with more enthusiasm than he could control.

"Is this for me?" Jason picked up the cup and took an appreciative sip. The coffee was still steaming. "Whoa. I didn't realise how much I needed that."

"Long day?"

"Yep. I've been on the go since six. I had my lunch at eleven-thirty, which is ridiculously early for me."

"That's for you too." Marc pushed a plate with a cookie on top towards him.

"You're a life saver." Jason broke the cookie in two and devoured half of it in two bites, before taking another sip of coffee.

Marc loved a man with a good appetite. Jack had been the same for most of their relationship. He'd always been the first to clear his plate at any meal and never refused an extra helping. Did Jason remind him of Jack? Physically, no. They were nothing alike, but there was something about his spirit that triggered a connection.

"What brings you into the city? Your factory is outside of town, right?" He dunked the rest of the cookie in his coffee then stuffed it in his mouth.

So, he's done his research on me too. "Meetings. A couple of potential clients and I had to see my accountant this morning too. Run-of-the-mill stuff, but it had to be done."

Jason nodded, picking up a napkin to wipe his mouth. "I try to leave most of that stuff to Ryman, though he makes me do my fair share of the boring work."

"You two are full partners?"

"We are, but Ryman started the agency so it's only fair we keep it in his name. I left the Navy around four years ago and started working for him. When he was looking for an investor to expand, I thought what the hell. Between my savings and a business loan I was able to join him."

Marc had suspected there was military discipline in Jason's background.

He pushed the second cookie across to him. "Have that. I'm not hungry anymore."

Jason looked at him with wide, hopeful eyes. "Only if you're sure."

"Take it."

He didn't need any further encouragement. Marc waited for him to finish. He tried not to stare, but he enjoyed watching Jason eat.

When was done he wiped his mouth and fingers. "I'm not usually a fan of sweet treats, but those are amazing." He took another drink of coffee to clear his mouth. "Now, I really need to tell you about what you came here for." Jason removed his jacket and rolled up his sleeves. Marc was drawn to his strong forearms and hands and suddenly imagined those hands roaming over his body.

As much as he wanted an update, Marc didn't want business talk to spoil the light, fun moment they were sharing. *Get a grip, Glass. You're paying him to find out what happened to Theo, not to sit there looking handsome for you to gawp over.*

"What have you got?"

"Well, I'm pretty sure there's something to be learnt from Soloman Archer. It might not be what we're hoping for, but the people at his office guard him like lions. He's got this PA called Chantelle and nothing will get past her without approval."

"Is that so unusual? He's an MP after all. They must hear from all kinds of nutters on a daily basis. It will be her job to protect him from them."

"True, but when I mentioned your brother's name, she knew who I was talking about."

"So, you've been to his office? Or did you talk to her on the phone?"

Jason told him what had happened when he'd called to see Soloman Archer. How the MP was out of town and his staff had blocked all attempts to speak with him. "She hid it well, Chantelle. When I mentioned Theo's name she was stoney-faced, but I saw the flicker of recognition. She knew who he was. Which means she's hiding something on behalf of her boss. Which means it's highly likely that your brother wasn't just bragging when he told you he had a relationship with Soloman Archer. I just don't have any proof yet."

Marc nodded. He reached under the table and produced a laptop, an iPad and a notebook from his briefcase. "You might find something in these. I should have brought them in at the start of the investigation, but I didn't know whether you would take the case then. Theo's passwords are all written down in the back of the book. I've highlighted the ones you need to gain access."

"Have you looked through these yourself?"

"Only briefly. I've told you before, I don't really want to watch my brother's sex tapes."

"Not a problem," Jason said. He lifted all three and slid them into his leather satchel. "I'll go through them and see what they can tell us. Your brother wasn't stupid. I'm sure he'll have protected himself with some kind of evidence."

It was a relief to hear Jason talk about Theo in such an open and matter-of-fact way, without judgement. Marc struggled to admit it, but he was ashamed of what his brother had been doing when he was alive. Marc hadn't been involved in the celebrity circuit in years, but it would reflect badly on him if it all came out. He hated himself for feeling that way. Theo was dead, he shouldn't hold a grudge against him now, but he couldn't stop that needling little voice that said it would destroy his reputation.

"Probably the biggest breakthrough I've had so far is with the men Theo shot his adult content with," Jason said. "I reached out to a bunch on the night after our meeting, and I've heard back from four so far. One of them lives right here in Blyham and has agreed to talk to me. Tonight." He took out his phone, pulled up a photo, and handed it to Marc.

It showed a very good-looking black man in his late twenties with a great smile.

"That's Dan," Jason continued. "He uses the name Cummer X when he's making sexual content. He's got a Hot-4-Fans account of his own and would frequently team up with Theo to shoot videos. They would share the costs of filming and editing and then post the clips on their respective accounts."

Marc stared at the picture and nodded. He was naïve when it came to all this stuff. He'd never subscribed to any of the online sex sites. He didn't even have any personal social media accounts. When it came to watching porn, he was old-school, and opted for the stash of DVDs he and Jack had collected over the years, the most recent of which was probably ten years old.

"He manages a gym in the West End of the city," Jason went on. "The whole content creation thing is just a side hustle. Why not, eh? When you're in a job that keeps your body in peak condition, might as well make a little something on the side."

That was one way of looking at it. "How long did he know Theo?"

"They were working together for the best part of a year before Theo's death. They always used the same cameraman and editor too. Dan is going to give me his contact details."

"What else has he told you?"

"Very little. I spoke to him for around two minutes this afternoon when he was on a break. I've arranged to meet him tonight when he finishes his shift. He'll be able to tell me a lot more then."

"Did you mention Soloman Archer?"

"I did."

"And?"

"He said he'd tell me about him later."

Marc gazed at the image again. Dan looked like any regular guy. His smile was friendly. His eyes were warm. Maybe he and Theo could have made a good couple. They could have sorted their lives out and made each other happy without the escorting and adult films.

"I want to come with you," he said, returning the phone.

"Not a good idea."

"I don't care. He's the first person who knows anything about Theo's private life. I want to hear what he has to say for myself."

"He's only expecting me. He might clam up or not talk at all if there's someone with me."

"It's a chance we'll have to take, because I'm coming."

* * * *

Jason wasn't happy with the idea, but Marc had insisted. He was due to meet Dan at ten-fifteen, after the gym closed. Jason gave Marc his home address and told him to pick him up just before ten.

With time to kill, Marc hung around the concert hall until it began to fill up with music-lovers for the evening show. He drove across the river and went for a quiet dinner at Chez Michelle's, a reliable café bar in the centre of the city, where he often dined with his parents. He paid little attention to what he ate. His mind was a mess of information, making wild connections about his brother and what he might have been involved with. He doubted the wisdom of what he was doing. Could anything be gained by digging into Theo's past like this? Maybe he should have left it all to Nadine Smythe. She'd likely have her story already. Jason had tracked Dan down quickly enough. There was a good chance Nadine had spoken to him already.

Later, he collected Jason from a modern apartment building on the river side. Not the kind of place he'd have thought he would live in. What *had* he expected? A seedy flat with a vermin problem and leaking roof, like some down-at-heel detective in an old movie? Marc was starting to realise that his reflections on the world were from another era.

Heavy rain pelted the roof of the car as he pulled up outside. Jason hurried from beneath the canopy of his building and dived into the passenger seat. He'd changed into jeans and a bomber jacket. His hair was soaked when he closed the door. He raked his fingers through it, pushing it back from his brow.

"Another shitty night," he commented. "I thought we were going to get a break from the rain for just one day."

"No such luck," Marc said, pulling into the traffic. "Where are we going?"

Jason gave the directions. Blyham was a small city, more like Leeds or York than a sprawling metropolis such as London or Birmingham. Though he was unfamiliar with the area, with Jason's guidance they reached the west side in less than ten minutes. It would have been sooner were it not for the atrocious road system. Marc was certain they changed the one-way routes on a monthly basis. Whenever he came into Blyham, he rarely took the same route twice.

"This is it," Jason said as they pulled into a narrow street.

They were in the old industrial quarter, a mishmash of warehouses, cheap cafés and wholesalers. The sign above the door for Hammer's gym didn't inspire confidence. The windows were blacked out, but Marc already had an image of bare wooden floors, boxing bags and basic free weights. This was not the kind of air-conditioned, well-equipped gym he was used to at the local leisure centres and hotels.

"He told me it was rough," Jason said, as though reading his mind. "I suspected as much, given where we are."

"Do you think he's on the level?" Considering the exterior of the building, Marc suspected the kind of man who worked here had to be some kind of hustler.

"He was sincere enough on the phone. I'll have a better idea when I speak to him face to face, but he seemed to have a genuine affection for your brother. I think they were good friends."

Good friends who happened to fuck each other on camera.

Marc chastened himself. He had to get over these starchy opinions he had of sex workers.

He had parked right in front. Jason jumped out and rushed through the rain to get inside. Marc followed him quickly.

First impressions lived up to his suspicions. The interior must have been a warehouse space at some point, and little had changed. The floors were covered in cheap board, giving a strong odour of woodchip and damp. The equipment looked ancient. Lots of plastic-covered benches with free weights and iron racks beside them. There were three treadmills against one wall, two of which were hung with 'Out of Order' signs. A couple of rickety-looking cycling machines and a boxing bag in the far corner completed the inventory of gym gear.

He was already suspicious that the real business behind this front was a supply in steroids and under-the-counter supplements.

A mop and red plastic bucket had been abandoned at the top end of the room. A quarter of the floor was wet around it, accounting for some of the damp smell.

"Hello," Jason hollered. His voice was clear and commanding in the austere surroundings. "Hello, Dan? It's Jason Durham, we spoke on the phone earlier."

There was no reply.

"The door was unlocked," Marc said. "He must have been expecting you."

"Must be out the back." They progressed across the floor and Jason called out again. Still no answer.

Marc wondered why he had insisted on coming. Investigation work was not like in the films. There was clearly a lot of time wasted in pursuit of dead-ends. He should have left this to the professional and focused on his own business.

Apart from their feet on the wooden boards, the place was silent.

"Maybe he's at the toilet," Marc suggested.

Jason took out his phone and dialled.

Marc jumped when he heard a loud ringing from the top of the room, from beyond an open door. Jason headed straight in that direction, and he followed. There was something purposeful and determined about Jason's movements.

They followed the ringing into a small storeroom. The shelves were stacked with towels, enormous bottles of vitamins and spare equipment. Marc was so busy taking it in that he walked straight into Jason's back, not realising he had stopped.

"What's the ma—"

The first thing he noticed was the blood. It covered the floor in a wide slick.

He followed its trail.

A man lay slumped against the shelves, his legs splayed in front of him. His head hung at an awkward angle. His black skin had taken on an ashy-grey hue. The front of his once-white T-shirt was a sodden, maroon-coloured mess.

"Oh, my God." Marc's voice sounded blank in his own ears. For a second he doubted that what he was looking at was real. That this moment was even happening.

But the wetness and the smell brought it all back into focus.

This was no hallucination. It was devastatingly real.

Chapter Six

The Scent of Death

Jason knew death when he saw it. It was something that had been emblazed on his mind so many times, he knew it far too well. The look, the presence, the smell. It never got any easier.

Marc pushed against his shoulder, trying to get around him. Jason raised an arm to block his way. "Stay back. You'll contaminate the scene."

"We have to help him," Marc said.

"We can't."

"It might not be too late."

The catch in Marc's voice, his natural instinct to do something good, struck a chord, but it was hopeless in this case. "We can't," Jason said firmly. "It's too late."

Marc gave a sharp intake of breath. "He's dead?"

There was nothing Jason could do for Dan Blumel now except preserve the crime scene. Leave his body untouched so the police forensic team could do their job. What he could do was make it easier on Marc. He turned around and put both hands on his shoulders. Marc's body trembled. His lips drew back from his teeth in twisted anguish. "Come on," Jason said, keeping his voice calm, firm but kind. He edged Marc towards the door. It seemed to work. Marc stopped resisting and moved back into the gym.

"Don't touch anything," Jason told him. "It's best that we return to the car, okay."

Marc was frozen for a second, and Jason was about to repeat himself when he nodded. Jason put a hand on his back and encouraged him to the front door. As they moved through the gym, Jason's eyes searched every corner of the room, behind each piece of equipment as they passed. Dan had not been dead for long, he was certain of that. Just minutes before they had arrived. The floor he'd been mopping was still wet. Either whoever had slaughtered him had fled the scene when they pulled up, or they were still in here. He'd put money on the first option but wasn't about to take a risk when Marc was with him.

They made it to the car. Jason told Marc to lock the doors then he called the police.

The rain clattered on the roof and obscured the view as they waited.

"He's...he's been stabbed." Marc's hand was on his face, agitatedly roaming across his chin.

"Almost certainly." The bloody T-shirt had masked the injuries, but there was no other explanation for such a severe bleed-out. From his appearance alone, Jason guessed he'd been stabbed multiple times. Whoever was responsible for the attack had done it in a frenzy.

"Because of us?" Marc looked at him across the dark interior of the car.

"Not necessarily." *Though it's a huge coincidence that it happens on the exact same night he chose to talk to us.* "There could be all kinds of reasons."

"Like what?"

"A disgruntled employee or a customer. Jealous partner. Drug dealers. You saw that place. It doesn't look like the most reputable gym in the city."

"But Theo was killed. And now the first person prepared to talk about what happened to him is also dead. It's… There's a connection… There must be."

"You're jumping to conclusions without evidence."

"But if I hadn't insisted on digging all of this up…"

"You're not responsible for this. Get that idea out of your head because it will only fester. Do you hear me? You hired me to find evidence. And right now, I don't have any. So, we have nothing to connect the two deaths."

Marc did not reply. They sat in silence.

Jason heard the sirens before the blue lights rounded the corner and two police cars pulled in front of them.

"Stay in the car," Jason told him. "I'll talk to them."

But by the time he'd got out, Marc was beside him on the pavement. Neither of them cared about getting wet and Jason didn't argue with him.

Four uniformed officers approached. Jason gave them a concise account of what they had found. A moment later, an ambulance arrived.

"You didn't try to administer first aid?" the lead constable asked.

"There was no point. He was already dead."

"And how do you know that if you didn't check?"

"I'm ex Royal Navy Police," he answered flatly. "He was dead."

Two of the officers went inside, followed by paramedics. Jason and Marc sheltered in the doorway of the building next door as the inevitable procedure unfolded. A police van arrived, and a barrier was erected in front of the gym. One of the constables, a stout young woman, came over to take their initial statements.

"Why were you here after closing time?" she asked.

There was no point in hiding the truth. They would see soon enough from Dan's phone records that they had been in touch.

"He agreed to talk to me about a case I'm investigating. It was just a routine interview," he added. "Dan thought he could help us out."

"You'd never met him before?"

"No, only on the phone."

He was aware of Marc beside him, shivering. It could have been from the cold, but he was just as likely to be in shock.

"Do you mind if we wait in the car?" he asked after a giving a very brief summary, leaving out the details of his case. "We won't go anywhere. Just to get out of the rain."

She nodded and they hurried back to the vehicle.

"Why didn't you tell them about Theo?" Marc asked.

"I will. But it's not important at the minute. They'll want a more detailed statement from us later. I'll decide what to tell them then."

"Why keep it secret?"

He exhaled. A long and weary sound. "Blyham police...it's best to keep them at arm's length."

"You said you used to be police yourself."

"Royal Navy Police," he corrected. "Not the same, but I know enough about policing to know this lot are not to be trusted. They're not all bad. There are some good officers on the force. But it's rotten too. And when it comes to dealing with minorities, it's got to be one of the worst in the country. You must have seen how badly they fucked up the Blyham Strangler case. How many men died before they took the threat seriously? Even then, they didn't actually find the killer through police work, it was some potential victims and members of the public who caught the bastard."

Marc watched him from the dark of the car. "What does that have to do with the murder tonight?"

"I would have thought it was obvious. It's three months since your brother died and they haven't brought in a single suspect for the hit-and-run. What does Theo have in common with the Blyham Strangler victims?"

Marc seemed to struggle with the answer, until, "He was gay."

"Exactly. If I know this lot, they'll have filed his case a few days after the crash, and no one will have bothered with it since. And now Dan, a gay sex worker. Black too. They won't know how fast to write this off as a drug debt or gang vendetta and move on. But if they think we came to see Dan in connection with Theo, they'll come down on us heavy. Especially if they find out we're also interested in a certain politician."

"So, we're going to say nothing?"

"We're going to say just enough."

The windows were misting up. Jason wiped the condensation with his sleeve to get a better look.

"Turn on the engine to get this clear," he said.

When visibility improved, he took in the latest scene. A plain clothes detective had arrived and was speaking to the uniformed officers. A PC pointed at Marc's car and the detective turned to look, before entering the building.

"Well, at least that's something," he said, recognising the attending officer. "Benito Coppola. Detective sergeant."

"You know him?"

"A bit. He's one of the better ones. Conscientious. He does care about the victims. Unfortunately, he's also brutally ambitious, which means he does what he's told from above. He's probably just the duty officer tonight. I doubt he'll be involved in the case beyond managing the crime scene until CID come in tomorrow."

Marc let out a long, mournful sigh and slumped back in his seat. He closed his eyes. In the dim light of the car, he appeared to have aged ten years.

"Are you all right?"

He kept his eyes closed and shook his head. "How can anyone be all right, after this."

Jason put a hand on his brow. His skin was clammy and cold. "You need to get out of here and get dry. Give me a few minutes to clear it and we'll be off."

Jason got out of the car. The rain was heavier than before and colder too. He hurried over to the cordon and wasted no time arguing with the PC standing guard.

"I'm one of the witnesses," Jason asserted. "I want to talk to DS Coppola. *Now.*"

After speaking into his radio, the stoney-faced PC raised the cordon tape and Jason ducked under.

DS Benito Coppola met him just inside the door. Benito was in his mid-thirties, very handsome with dark, Italian looks. He wasn't Jason's type, but he'd always had a strong respect for him as the only openly gay officer he was aware of on the Blyham police force. Unfortunately, his intent to climb the greasy pole all the way to the top kept Jason from ever fully trusting him.

"Is there anything else you need from us?"

"What's your hurry?" Benito asked, eyeing him suspiciously.

"Marc is in shock. He's not handling it well, and he's also soaked to the skin. I need to get him somewhere dry and warm. We've already given our statements."

Benito tilted his head, a smirk hovering on his lips. "Your statement raises more questions than it answers."

"I told your officer everything that happened from the moment we arrived. We didn't see anyone else in the building and no one left after we went back outside. Whoever did this was either long gone when we got here, or there's a back way out."

"You were here on an investigation? What's it about?"

"I'm looking for information on someone that Dan used to know. He told me to drop by after his shift and he'd tell me what he could. It was nothing important. Clearing up a few details, that's all."

Benito's face was emotionless. He stared at Jason. Oldest trick in the book. Create an uncomfortable silence until the target feels compelled to fill it with more information. Jason returned the stare, his lips pressed tight. He could play this game as well as anyone.

"Ah, fuck it," Benito said at last. "Take him home. But make sure you're both available tomorrow morning. Someone will be in touch to take a fuller statement. And it had better be more worthwhile than the bullshit you've given us tonight."

"Will do," he said, attempting to put some reverence into his voice while having none.

Jason hurried back to the car and Marc.

Chapter Seven

Urgent Relief

It was after two when Marc pulled up in front of Jason's apartment building. Neither of them had said much on the drive back from the gym.

"How do you feel now?" Jason asked.

Marc kept his hands on the wheel and stared out of the window at the quiet street. "Honestly?" he released a huge sigh. "I have no fucking idea. Numb. Frazzled. Wired. Exhausted."

"Yes," Jason said. "Me too."

They sat in silence again. Jason made no move to get out of the car and Marc was in no rush to hurry him on. The prospect of driving home to the empty house was something he'd rather delay. At last, he turned to face Jason. His face was set in a grim expression. "I could do with a drink," Marc said. "Is anywhere around here still open?"

"Not tonight," Jason said. "Pull around the corner and you can park. I've got plenty of booze upstairs."

He followed Jason inside and they took the elevator to the seventh floor. The apartment was much as Marc had imagined from these new developments, with a large open plan kitchen and living area. The curtains were open, revealing a small balcony. The lights of the opposite bank glistened on the ink black river. Marc was in no mood to compliment the interior or the view.

Jason disappeared for a moment, before returning with a pile of towels. He handed one to Marc. "Give me your jacket. I'll hang it up to dry."

Marc suspected the wool-blend blazer was already ruined, but did what he was told, before rubbing the towel over his head. His feet were wet too. Without waiting for permission, he took off his socks and shoes and dried his cold toes with the towel.

Jason came back, minus his own jacket. His damp T-shirt clung to his torso. Despite everything that had happened tonight, Marc noticed his nipples, hard little bullets poking at the sodden cotton.

Jason went behind the counter and opened the fridge. "What do you want?"

"I'll take whatever you've got."

Jason pulled out a bottle of vodka and an ice tray. "I've got Coke or tonic," he said, dumping ice into two heavy crystal tumblers and half filling them with spirt. He put a tiny splash of Coke into his own glass before the putting the mixers on the top for Marc to help himself.

Marc's mind flashed on the memory of Dan lying dead in a pool of his own blood. He'd only ever seen one dead person before. That had been his husband on his hospital death bed, and later in the chapel of rest. Jack had died too soon, taken by a virus the government had allowed to get out of control, but Dan...*Jesus*. The terror that boy must have gone through in the moments before the end.

Marc ignored the mixers and took his drink neat. The vodka seared his throat on the way down, but he welcomed its fiery intensity.

Jason came out from the behind the counter and wandered to the window. Rain lashed against the glass. "Will this ever fucking stop?" he mumbled, taking a deep swallow.

Marc took in the fine shape of his silhouette. His broad shoulders, tight middle and waist, his beefy butt. He wondered with indifference why he would even notice those things, then his mind leapt onto the next grim memory of Dan.

Marc and the family had been advised against seeing Theo's body after the crash. The police had other ways to identify him and had spared his nearest from that ordeal. Would Dan's family be given the same respect?

He joined Jason at the window. The nightscape of the city looked so serene.

"Somewhere out there is the killer." His voice sounded cold. Alien to his own ears.

"Undoubtedly. Unless they knew what they were doing and are already on their way back to London."

"To Soloman Archer, you mean? You think he sent a professional hitman to shut Dan up before he could talk to us?"

"I don't know what I think. I sure as fuck don't have any evidence. And without that, I have nothing." He opened his hand and blew away imaginary dust.

"What did that detective say when you spoke to him?"

"Benito? He didn't give anything away. Only that they want to see us tomorrow to give them a more detailed statement."

"And what will you say? About why we were there."

Jason shrugged. "I need to sleep on that one." He knocked off the rest of his drink and returned to the counter for a refill. Marc did the same.

His eyes were drawn again to Jason's nipples. The clinging T-shirt left little to the imagination, defining his shoulders and the broad slabs of his pectorals. He had strong biceps. He obviously worked out, but not to an obsessive degree. He looked beautifully fit rather than a gym fanatic. Marc questioned again why he should notice something like that after the horrors they'd experienced tonight.

He realised with alarm that Jason had caught him looking. His wide eyes stared directly at Marc, then lowered, as though checking him out too. Marc's pulse quickened. He picked up the glass and carried it back to the window. His hand trembled. He didn't want Jason to see that too.

"I wonder if they've told them yet," he said.

"Told who?"

"Dan's family. Have they received that dreadful knock at the door? The one that only means bad news."

"It's over four hours since we found him. The police are bound to have called on them by now. If they can be relied on to do their fucking job, that is."

"You don't like cops."

He heard the sound of Jason's footsteps on the floor behind him. His heart quickened. *Is this what I think it is? Or am I reading this all wrong?*

"You're shaking," Jason said, his voice was close.

"I don't think I've warmed up yet." The lie was desperate even to his own ears.

"What do I think of the police? In Blyham? Not a lot. After the last year, even less."

Although Marc didn't live in the city, he couldn't have escaped the horror of the Blyham Strangler, who had terrorised the LGBTQIA community for eighteen months. Six men had been murdered before he was caught. But he wasn't the only massive failure on the part of the local authorities. Hate crime had been on rise for a long time before he'd claimed his first victim, and the police had done little to curb it. Despite a sizeable gay village in the heart of the city, Blyham was one of the most dangerous places in the country for that community. *His* community.

Jason was close behind him. Marc could feel his breath on the back of his neck.

He wanted him. He hadn't been this attracted to a man since Jack had died. Marc hadn't been living a life of celibacy either, but all he was ever interested in was getting his rocks off and moving on. He didn't care about names or professions or getting to know anyone better than for what they had under their clothes. What made Jason so different?

Marc turned around. Jason was inches from his face. So handsome. His eyes glinting with the lights from the window.

"What—?"

Before he could form a question, Jason's face was up in his. Their lips touched. Then they were open, yielding against each other, tongues thrusting. Marc wrapped a fist around Jason's head and pulled him deeper into the kiss. Their beards and stubble rasped against their skins. The scent of his body, his cologne, the booze on his breath was intoxicating.

Marc was hard and it was clear to discern that Jason was too.

Jason had put down his drink. He grasped Marc's head in both hands, intensifying the passion and heat of the kiss. Finally, they broke away, panting in each other's faces. Skin flushed.

"Shouldn't be doing this," Jason growled. He pressed his cheek against Marc's. His tongue followed the line of his jaw, all the way to the ear.

"I don't care," Marc said. He dipped sideways to get rid of his glass, before going all in for Jason. His hands went straight for his jeans, tearing open his belt, riving at the fly buttons. Jason untucked Marc's shirt and slid underneath. Marc shivered as he ran his hands around his torso. No one had even touched him like this since Jack. With casual hook ups, Marc would bend them over, take them from behind and be on his way. This was more intimate. So much more intense. He hadn't even appreciated how desperate for sex he was.

He shoved Jason's jeans to his thighs. He grabbed his hips and realised Jason was wearing a jockstrap. He slipped around the back, cupping his bare arse. His cock was ignited further. He thought he would burst. With a deep groan, he tightened his grip on Jason's bare backside, pulling their hips together, crushing their raging cocks in between. There was a wetness in the front of his own underwear as he leaked pre-cum.

Jason forced his own hands down the back of Marc's trousers, straight into his briefs, to cup his butt. Marc groaned again. No one had been close to that in years, now he was letting Jason maul it like a prime piece of meat. It was so fucking hot.

Marc needed more. So much more.

He slid down Jason's body, pressing his face on his chest and belly, until he drew level with his dick. His pushed his cheek against the hard bulge. Jason's cock tented the front of his jock pouch. Marc turned his head, mouthing the outline. Pre-cum oozed through the white fabric. He caught the taste on his lips, and it inflamed him further.

Marc no longer knew himself as pulled the pouch aside to unleash Jason's beautiful cock. His was thick and uncircumcised. His sticky juices glistened on the folds of his foreskin. Marc sucked on the tip, trying to draw out every drop of precious moisture. The taste was salty, strong, incredible. He couldn't control himself. He gripped Jason's smooth balls and the root of his cock in one hand, guiding it into his mouth. Now Jason groaned and slid his fingers through Marc's hair, urging him to go further. He didn't need encouragement. Marc opened his mouth and took him all the way, until the blunt head of Jason's cock reached the back of his throat.

He was out of practice. Before his gag reflex ruined everything, he eased back, catching a breath through his nose, and took up a hurried motion. He was torn between wanting to explore and savour every hard inch of this beautifully smooth dick and the urge to let loose, to go wild and fill himself with cum.

He tugged Jason's jeans to his ankles, giving him the freedom to spread his knees and thrust into him. With one hand on his balls, he slipped the other around the back again, to enjoy that hot, bare arse. He slid his fingers into the tight crack, finding his hole. That molten hot opening.

Jason moaned, easing his cock back and forwards, seeming to enjoy every second as Marc sucked and slurped.

His breath hissed and he gripped Marc's head in both hands. "Easy. Easy. I'm not ready to end this yet."

Part of Marc wanted to continue, wanted to feel the hot gush of cum across his tongue and down his throat. A more dominant part of him wanted much more. He fell away, panting, staring at the magnificent and wet cock just inches from his face.

Jason toed off his shoes and out of his jeans. He hauled the T-shirt over his head and cast it across the room. Marc gazed upwards at his body. It was as fantastic as he'd imagined. Thickset and trim. Jason's hairy chest and treasure trail made his pulse race faster. Jason's sexy, gap-toothed smile beamed down at him.

"It's my turn to see you," he said.

Marc gave Jason's cock one last suck, before getting to his feet. He unbuttoned his shirt and let it drop. He was probably a good ten years older than Jason, but he had no worries about exposing his body. Running, boxing and swimming kept him in good shape for his age. He'd never look like a thirty-year-old again, but neither did he want to. Compared to Jason, the hair on his chest was relatively sparse, but his pecs were firm and well-shaped, and his belly was flat.

Jason murmured appreciatively. "Turn around."

Marc did what he asked. Suddenly Jason was behind him, pressing his chest into his back. The warm contact of skin of against skin caused Marc to shudder again. He was so out of practice with all of this. Jason reached around and unfasted his belt and trousers. They dropped to his ankles. Jason's hands were on his cock, smoothing the cotton of his briefs against the bulging outline. He nuzzled into the nape of Marc's neck, making him shiver all over.

"Do you like this?" Jason grazed his fingers down the length of his cock, finding his balls, teasing them through the light material.

Marc's stomach quivered. "Yes," he gasped.

Jason explored, moving both hands to his waist. Every touch provoked fresh sensations. Marc had neglected the sensual side of his nature for far too long. He knew Jack had never wanted him to lock himself away for the rest of his life, but Marc had done that anyway.

Jason tucked his fingers into the waist of his briefs and tugged them down, exposing his arse. Marc let out a long exhalation as Jason rubbed his wet cock against his cheeks. *Oh God, that feels so good.* Jason held his hips and ground his hardness against him. Marc surrendered, arching his spine to push back.

After all they'd been through tonight, having that cock inside him would make everything feel better.

"Put it in me," he growled.

Jason pressed his length into the cleft of his butt. "You sure?"

"Yes. Fuck me."

Jason stepped back and gave his arse a firm slap. "Stay right there." He hurried away.

Trembling, Marc struggled out of his wet trousers. He was naked when Jason returned moments later, carrying a bottle of lube, a strip of condoms and a towel.

"Get on the couch," Jason said. "Show me your arse."

Marc wasn't used to being ordered around, in his personal or professional life, but doing what Jason told him to do was a thrill. He climbed onto the sofa and rested his arms across the back, sticking out his butt for Jason's approval.

"Spread it," Jason said.

Marc reached back, opening his cheeks. He had a good arse. His exercise regime saw to that, and he kept the crack clean and manscaped. He gasped as Jason dribbled cold lube into the cleft, then massaged it around his opening, before pushing his finger inside.

"Oh, God." Marc rested against the back of the sofa and breathed deeply. He was tight. No surprise after all this time, but he wanted to go through with this more than anything. He focused on his sphincter and willed it to relax.

Jason applied plenty of lube and slid a finger all the way to the knuckle. He paused, giving Jason time to adjust, before withdrawing and going back in with two fingers. He worked his hole with a slick, twisting motion, getting him prepared. His nails were short and there was no pain or scratching.

Marc could barely wait for Jason to put on a condom. *I need this. I need him.*

"All right," Jason said, manoeuvring into position.

"Do it," he urged.

After so many years, it was like losing his virginity all over again. As Jason's cock pushed against his resistance, Marc was sure he would never be able to take it. Jason was too big for him. They should have spent longer warming up. Marc's hole stretched and stretched. Wider. Wider. He was going to break. He bit his lip to keep from calling out for Jason to stop. *You want this. Take it.*

Then he was through. Jason's blunt head passed through his sphincter and the rest was easy. He slid deep until his hips pressed against Marc's butt. He leaned over, kissing the side of his face.

"You okay?"

Marc nodded, heart pounding in his chest. There was no pain, no ache, just pleasure.

"Fuck me," he demanded. "Let me have it all."

Jason withdrew until just the head remained inside, then he gripped Marc's hips and shoved all the way back. They worked up to a quick rhythm. As Jason rammed into him, Marc shoved back. The room was filled with the crack of skin against skin and their guttural cries of passion and desperate hunger. *Holy shit.* Marc gritted his teeth. In seconds he'd been transported to a plane of pleasure he'd forgotten even existed. The feeling of fullness, of being stuffed by another man, took away all the stress of the last few hours. They found assurance and support in each other's bodies.

How could he have forgotten all the pleasure his arse could provide.

Jason put a hand on the small of his back as he fucked. Every touch was like electric, triggering sparks of delight all through his body. They were connected. Afterwards they might feel shame, even regret, that the death of a young man had brought them to this, but right now, they needed each other. They needed this.

Marc's sensations were so strong and heightened that he came without touching himself.

"Oh, God." His words were strained as pleasure gripped his body and he pumped cum over Jason's sofa. His orgasm seemed endless. As it surged through his body, causing paroxysms, the sudden tightening of his sphincter triggered Jason's release. He buried his cock deep inside him as he shuddered and spurted.

Marc set himself against the back of the sofa as Jason collapsed across him. They panted and gasped, their bodies hot and wet with sweat.

Outside, the torrential rain continued to rattle against the window.

And somewhere in the night, a man was dead, and a killer roamed free.

Chapter Eight

Night Talk

They lay in bed, listening to the rain. Exhausted but far from sleep. Jason was propped on one elbow, gazing at Marc who lay on his back. He was even more handsome than before. His cheeks were flushed with sex, and some of the tension had eased in his brow. Jason didn't know where to begin processing any of this. Fucking a client was as unprofessional as it was possible to get. Ryman would have a shit fit when he learnt about this. And yet tonight, after what they'd discovered, it had seemed like the right thing to do. The only thing to do.

Having Marc in bed beside him, that was the best thing ever. Jason had been surprised when Marc had asked to stay, saying he didn't fancy spending the rest of the night alone. Most guys couldn't wait to get going once they'd shot their load. In the majority of cases, Jason couldn't wait to get rid of them either. Not Marc.

"Why did you leave the Navy?" Marc asked.

Jason hesitated, then turned to look at him.

"Sorry. None of my business. I shouldn't have asked."

Jason put a hand on his chest. "It's fine. It's not a big deal. I'm not used to talking about myself, that's all. I left because it was time. When I joined the Navy police, it was a dream come true. I loved it. I served in places all over the world, but I got shot in the leg while on duty, nothing major, you can barely see the scar now the hair has grown over it. But after that I started to feel homesick and pined for England. I spent my last year serving in ports all over the UK but that still wasn't enough. It wasn't England I was desperate to return to, it was Blyham."

"Wow. Not many people can lay claim to that." Marc's tone was completely deadpan.

Jason chuckled. "I guess not. If you told me that when I was twenty-five, I'd have pissed myself laughing. Said there was no chance I'd ever come back here. I guess, I changed. We all do."

"You were shot."

"We were sent to arrest a senior officer who had taken to the bottle and beaten a cadet so badly he was in hospital. He was pissed as a fart when we turned up and the gun went off. I was lucky — no serious damage, and the bullet went right through. But it was the moment that caused me to rethink my career."

"So, you became a private investigator."

"That was stroke of luck. I came to work for Ryman on a casual basis and loved it straight away. When he started looking for investment to expand the business, it made sense for me put in and become a partner with him."

Marc rolled onto his side. Beneath the covers, his hand slipped over Jason's waist. Jason shuffled down so they were facing each other.

"I didn't know the first thing about private detectives," Marc said. "I did an internet search for agencies in Blyham, and you came out top."

"That's because we're the best." They both laughed. "You know, I'm going to have to hand over your case to Ryman in the morning. He won't let me continue when he finds out about this."

Marc's smile faded. "Who's going to tell him?"

"I'll have to. This breaks all the rules. I can't continue after tonight."

"I want you to. I don't want Ryman. You know the case. You've done all the work. I want you to keep going with it. Ryman won't understand all the things my brother was into. He'll likely freak out."

"He's more open-minded than you'd think. And has a lot of empathy."

"I freaked out about a lot of this stuff myself. Trust me, he's not going to get it the way you do." Marc moved closer. "Don't tell him. Please."

Jason was uneasy. Trust was at the forefront of their working relationship. Ryman might never trust him again if he learnt about this later. And yet, he didn't want to let go of the case. He hadn't been all that keen on taking it to begin with, but he was one hundred percent invested in it now. Even more so now that another young man had died. Jason didn't believe in crackpot conspiracy theories about the MP and a cover-up, but there were too many coincidences to ignore.

"All right, I'll stay on it. But we can't do this again. Not if I'm going to pretend to Ryman that nothing happened."

Marc rolled onto his back. He put his hand behind his head and stared at the ceiling. "All right," he said at last.

It hurt to feel him pull away and withdraw, but it was exactly what Jason had just asked him to do. He flipped onto his own back, staring at the shadows above. "Tell me more about Theo."

"Like what? You probably know him better than I do now. I didn't have nerve to go through any of his online stuff."

"The adult content is all Hart Stone," Jason corrected. "That's not the real Theo. Tell me about your brother."

Marc sucked his breath through his teeth. "I still don't think I ever knew him. We were so many years apart. When he was little, I thought he was a bratty kid. Then when he was a teenager, he thought I was a boring old fart. The only time he ever took an interest in what I did was when I was on *The Partnership*. Reality TV was everything to Theo, so me being on the telly for a couple of months made me hot stuff. But afterwards, he hated me for it. He applied to go on different shows and kept getting rejected. He once had a rant and asked me 'What the fuck have you got that I don't?' Maybe if we'd been closer in age, we would have got on a lot better. I'd have looked after him, kept his feet in the ground and out of the clouds."

"I've only been investigating a few days, but from what I've discovered so far, I don't think Theo was unhappy. What he did for a living might seem unconventional to some, but he appeared to enjoy it. And he was good at it."

Marc's brow furrowed.

"I mean it," Jason said. "There's a professionalism to Theo's videos that I don't see in many of the others. I've had to look into the accounts of the men he worked with, and the majority of it is bargain basements stuff, filmed on a phone. On the whole, Theo used a cameraman, and his stuff is well lit and thought out. The other guys, well, the stuff they shot with Theo is by far their best work."

"It's still porn though, however well made."

He wondered what Marc's problem really was. He'd just proved that it wasn't sex. So, why was he so against sex work? Was it just because it was his brother?

"Theo had a lot more subscribers than the other guys. Six or seven times more than some of them. A lot of people haven't even cancelled their subscriptions, despite the fact there is no new content."

Marc lurched up. "What the fuck? You mean people are still tossing off over him, even though he's dead?"

Jason spoke calmly. It wouldn't help to get Marc riled up now. "I've submitted requests to all the sites he had an active profile with to have his accounts closed. I'm not sure how long that's gonna take. The ones that involve a paid subscription, I imagine will be soon. And I found the passwords for his social media accounts in the notebook you gave me, so they're already gone. But there's no way to remove it all. People download and share things. Some of it is going to stay on the internet forever."

"Ah, shit." Marc got into a sitting position and raised his knees. He put his head in his hands. "What have I done? Poking around is only going to make it worse. If the press makes a connection between Dan and Theo, it's going to encourage people to go searching for it all over again."

"Not necessarily. This sounds harsh, but a young man murdered in an inner-city gym is not going to gather that much interest. I'll be surprised if Dan's death gets more than a few paragraphs in the local papers.

Look at what happened with the Blyham Strangler. No one gave a shit until the sixth man was killed."

"That doesn't make it right."

"Of course it doesn't. What I mean is, I don't think anyone is going to make the connection to Theo. Blyham police are so shit I doubt they'd bother investigating even if they did."

Marc's breath quickened. He flung back the covers and got out of bed. He paced the floor, running his hands through his hair, before searching for his clothes.

Jason got up and went to him. "You don't have to go," he said, and tried to put his arms around him. Marc stepped aside and retrieved his underwear, stepping into them.

"I can't breathe. I can't think." His trousers hung over the back of a chair. He pulled them off and put them on.

"I'm sorry," Jason said. "I've upset you. I shouldn't have said—"

"It's not you. It's this whole fucked-up situation. I thought I could control it, by getting ahead of Nadine's story, but all I've done is make it worse."

"You haven't."

"Haven't I? That man is dead. He would still be alive if we hadn't gone to speak to him."

Jason fought to speak softly. "It likely has nothing to do with us. Or with Theo. Dan could have been involved in all kinds of shady business."

"But he also knew things about Theo. And if we hadn't pressed him on it, he might still be alive."

"No one knew we were going to see him tonight. I doubt very much that he tipped off Theo's killer he was going to talk. You're making massive jumps here, with no evidence to back it up."

There was a pained expression on Marc's face. He bared his teeth and fastened his shirt. Jason realised that talking it through was only making him worse. He reached for him, putting a hand on his arm, but Marc shrugged him off.

"I need to go home. I need space to think."

"Okay. Are you sure you're all right to drive? Let me make you a cup of tea or a coffee first, eh?"

"I don't need anything."

How had they gone from such a moment of intimacy to this vast, cold distance? Jason opened a drawer and put on a pair of pyjama bottoms while Marc finished dressing. Anything he said now would only make the situation worse. He went into the kitchen and poured a shot of vodka. He knocked it down neat.

Marc came through a moment later, carrying his jacket.

"Are your clothes dry?" Jason asked.

"Still damp." There was weary tone to his voice. "Doesn't really matter. I'll get soaked going to the car anyway."

"You don't have to go," Jason said, trying again.

"I want to."

The words hit like a punch. "Be careful then."

Marc nodded and made straight for the door. "See you," he said, letting himself out.

The flat was eerily quiet afterwards.

Fuck. How did that go so wrong?

Jason poured another drink. Marc's emotions and feelings about his brother's death and their relationship were obviously problematic and painful. More deeply rooted than Marc probably realised himself.

Fucking him had been a mistake. Huge. It had complicated an already complex situation.

In all likelihood, Marc would fire him in the morning. Then he'd have to admit to Ryman the reason why.

Fuck. Fuck. Fuck.

Jason knocked off the shot and went back to bed. Tomorrow could not be any worse than today.

Chapter Nine

Suspicions

Jason hadn't heard from Marc when he reached the office the next day. He took his silence as an indicator that he hadn't been fired and continued to work on the case. He felt like shit. The lack of sleep combined with too many shots of vodka before bed had resulted in a stinking hangover and he didn't get to work until almost nine-thirty.

Olivia was already at her desk.

"Is Ryman in?" he asked.

"Not until midday. He's serving papers down in Durham and is meeting a client afterwards."

At least he wouldn't have to face his partner and deliver an update on the unexpected twist the case had taken. He made cups of tea for Olivia and himself and went into his office.

He'd been right about one thing. Dan's murder had featured fourth on the morning's local news update and hadn't made it into any of the newspapers, though it would have occurred after they went to press anyway. Dan's name hadn't been mentioned on the news and his gut instinct was that, unless there was of dearth of other things to report, it wouldn't go much further. It was a miserable fact of modern times that the murder of a single young black man didn't warrant a lot of attention from the mainstream media.

Jason opened the contacts on his phone and skimmed through. It had only struck him on that drive in that he might have a source of information. He scrolled to C. *Bingo*. Benito Coppola. The DS who'd been at the scene last night. Jason had helped the police out with an assault case about fifteen months ago. He'd saved Benito's details in case they should ever come in handy. Today was that day.

Benito answered after five rings. "I'm off duty," he grumbled. "About to go to bed. I was on night shift, remember?"

"Sorry," Jason said. "I didn't appreciate the time."

"So, what is it? Did you suddenly remember something you forgot to tell us last night?"

"Sarcasm doesn't suit you," Jason said, giving it maximum charm. "I take it you're not involved in the case."

"Picked it up when I was on duty. My part is done. You need to contact C.I.D. to speak to the officers involved."

"You must have checked out the CCTV. Did that confirm what we told you?"

A sigh. "It did. We've got you arriving and leaving at exactly the time you said."

"And there I was, thinking you didn't believe me."

"I don't believe anything anyone says until I have evidence for it."

"Wise man. So, what else does the footage show? You've got the killer or killers on camera, right?"

Benito laughed. "Whose investigation is this? I'm not going to tell you anything."

Jason turned the charm up higher. "Oh, come on. I just need to know if this is connected to something I'm looking into."

"The mysterious person Dan was going to give you information about?"

"That's right."

"You're a lying bastard."

"Did it look like a gang feud? That's all I need to know."

There was a long pause before Benito said. "Someone came in ten minutes before you did. Dressed all in black and wearing a balaclava." He hung up before Jason could ask anything else.

Jason stared into space. Well, it certainly sounded like a gang hit. But these days, most gangs were armed with guns. They were cold and efficient. The knife attack on Dan had been frenzied. Jason could see from the extent of Dan's injuries that he'd been stabbed multiple times. That didn't sound like bad business. It was more personal.

The killer had got there just after ten when the gym closed. If he and Marc had been early, they would have walked in on it. And what? Been able to stop it? Become victims themselves? *Damn it. What the fuck is going on?*

His gut told him the two cases were connected, but how? There was no way the killer could have known Dan was about to talk to them about Theo, unless Dan had told them himself. And even so, what had Dan known that was so important it had cost him his life?

Soloman Archer? It seemed a likely fit. Theo had been escorting for Soloman... Maybe it went further than that. Maybe Dan was involved too. Threesomes? Sex parties? How many other guys might Soloman have paid for sex?

Jason pulled up his list of the men he'd so far identified as working with Theo. Trace Grey had already told him to "get to fuck" and had blocked him on all his social media accounts. Trace, whoever he was, had something to hide. He'd spoken briefly with another two men, but they had both said their sessions with Theo had been one-time deals. Neither of them was local to Blyham, and one of them had been living in Berlin for seven months. He checked whether any of the other models he'd contacted had replied and there was nothing new. Fine. The next step was to find out their real identities. It was never as easy to identify someone's IP address as it appeared on TV, but it wasn't impossible either.

He spent the next hour gathering all the relevant information available on the guys Theo had worked with, and once the bundle was ready he sent it to Brody, the IT wizard the firm used when they needed something fast. Jason had never met Brody in person. Ryman had assured him it was better that he didn't. Brody's methods and the systems he had access to weren't one hundred percent legal, but he got results. They billed his services as a maintenance expense for the office software system.

Jason checked his case notes again. He'd written camera operator and drawn a big circle around it. *Yes.* That had to be the next important step. He'd already pointed out to Marc that Theo's videos were of a far higher quality than those of his peers. His clips were first rate. That level of professionalism couldn't be achieved with a couple of iPhones, a selfie light and a friend who didn't mind getting into intimate places. Theo had had help.

None of the sex work models credited their camera people. Jason guessed that was because they had more mainstream work and didn't want to be blacklisted from the wedding and christening market for shooting porn on the side. It was the next line of enquiry worth pursuing. Dan had even promised to give him the contact details for their regular guy. No chance of that now.

Jason opened a search engine and started looking at all the professional photographers in Blyham.

* * * *

Marc's statement was taken by an unsmiling Detective Sergeant with a grey pallor and a combover the like of which Marc hadn't seen since the 1990s. Marc had called the station earlier that morning and arranged a time between meetings when he could attend. He'd considered contacting Jason first, to arrange doing the interview together, but after the way they had left things last night, he hadn't known what to say, so had said nothing.

When he'd first woken up after less than three hours' sleep, he'd intended to call the agency and cancel the case. He'd pay for the work that had been done already and leave it at that. By the time he'd gone for a run, taken a shower and managed some breakfast, he'd changed his mind. The truth was he didn't know how he felt, and it was never a good idea to make a decision from a place of uncertainty.

Marc had pushed the Jason situation aside and got on with the day.

He might have been able to forget about Jason for a few hours, but he couldn't get the image of Dan Blumel out of his mind. Marc had gone through his first meeting that morning like a zombie, listening to what his managers had to report without taking in any details of what they'd said.

All he could think about was a dead boy on the floor of a third-rate gym.

"Just to clarify what you're saying," the DS made a show of rereading his notes. He'd taken down every word Marc had said in an illegible scrawl. "You went to the gym to speak to Dan Blumel about your brother."

"Yes."

"And you hired a private detective to find Blumel?" he made no attempt to conceal the disdain he had for the situation.

"I didn't hire him to find Blumel, no. I hired him to find out what happened to Theo. Dan was the first person to come forward with any information."

The DS regarded Marc over the rim of his spectacles, which were worn on a leather cord around his neck. "And what information was that?"

Marc struggled to keep his cool. This man, DS Thomson, was an arsehole and he was starting to understand Jason's contempt for the Blyham force. "I don't know, because we didn't get to talk to him. Maybe you would know something yourself if you'd bothered to interview Dan after my brother's death. Jason managed to track him down after a few days. You guys had three months to find him, and you didn't."

Thomson pushed the glasses up the bridge of his nose. "That's a separate matter. I'm interested in last night."

Marc took a deep breath. When he spoke, the hardness in his own voice surprised him. "It's hardly separate if trying to find out what happened to Theo is what took us to the gym. The only reason I've hired a private investigator is because your lot haven't done their job."

Thomson was about to reply when Marc cut him off. "I have to get back to work. I've given you my statement. Now let me sign it and maybe you can get on with solving this poor guy's death."

Thomson was indignant. "Your statement raises far more questions than it answers. We'll need to speak to you again."

"Speak to my lawyers—Booths and Co. If you want another statement from me, you can arrange it through them."

He pulled out his own pen, the special one he used for signing contracts, and scribbled his name across all four sheets of the police statement. Thomson didn't even meet his eye when he got up and left.

Marc was seething. Everything he'd heard and suspected about this force was true. They were a bunch of self-serving pricks. More interested in easy answers than any justice for the victims of crime or their families. If or when they discovered who was responsible for Theo's death, he would go to the press afterwards and call out every piece of shitty police work the officers in this station were accountable for.

The one thing he hated more than incompetence was laziness.

Marc's mood did not improve when he got outside. The rain that had held off for most of the morning had started again while he was in the station. He didn't feel like he'd been truly dry in over a week. He put up an umbrella and hurried towards his car. As he clicked the fob to unlock the doors, a figure stepped in front of him.

From the flash of blonde helmet hair beneath the umbrella, he knew who it was before he looked at her. Nadine Smythe.

"Helping the police with their enquiries, are you?" She stepped between Marc and the car.

"I've no doubt you've got a hotline to several of Blyham's finest, so you probably have a better idea of what went on in there than I do." He tried to move around her, but she was unbudgeable.

"It's more than a coincidence that days after you start an investigation into your brother's death, your first contact ends up dead before you can talk to them."

How the fuck did she know all that? "Are you investigating me? You seem to know a lot about my movements."

"I've got tabs all over this city."

"Then you have no reason to bother me."

Nadine was not to be shaken. She gripped his arm. "What's wrong with you? We're on the same side. If you weren't so pig-headed you would realise that. I want to solve Theo's murder as much as you do."

"But for very different reasons," he said. "You want a story. I want answers and justice."

"I want those things too," she said, trying a softer line. "I'm not your enemy, Marc. Instead of getting some backstreet investigator to root out the case, you could work with me. I'm onto something already. I'm this close to uncovering it." She held her thumb and index finger millimetres apart.

Marc might have been convinced, if his mind didn't flash on the lurid headlines she'd written about his husband and his brother. This was the woman who'd had a photographer follow him during a national pandemic in order to get pictures of him visiting his dying husband. If that wasn't enough, she'd intruded on his grief again when she'd trailed him at the restricted funeral he'd been forced to arrange. She was interested in sensationalism and nothing more meaningful than that.

"If you're so close to the truth, then you really don't need me."

Seeming to realise she was getting nowhere, she pushed on anyway. "You found the body last night. That fact alone makes you a person of interest. I have a duty to write that up."

He finally managed to walk around her. "Write what the hell you want." He sighed. "We both know you'll do that anyway. Your credibility as a journalist is in the sewer. Try having a sliver of respect and compassion for the victim's family this time."

"Get down off your bloody high horse," she snapped. "I'm trying to find out what happened to your brother. You could show a little gratitude."

Marc laughed. With that final comment she had lost the tiny fragment of credibility she might have had left.

He got into the car. Nadine was still talking when he shut the door in her face. He started the engine and drove away. She could follow him if she liked, the chances were high that she would, though she always knew where to find him anyway.

Nadine's ambush had helped him in a way she would never know. She'd made him remember the reason he'd gone to see Jason in the first place. He wanted to get to the truth before she did. He had a much greater chance of doing that with Jason on his side. Until twenty minutes ago, he'd been close to terminating their agreement.

Nadine had made him realise that he needed Jason Durham more than ever.

Chapter Ten

The Ex-boyfriend

Blyham Castle sat in the oldest quarter of the city, on a small peninsula jutting into the river Bly. It dated back to 1272 and had been designated a cultural World Heritage Site since 1985. Like many local people, Jason realised that he failed to appreciate the importance of such a historic building right on his doorstep. He'd first visited the castle on a school trip when he was thirteen years old and had been bored out of his mind. Then later, when he'd attended a wedding reception in the main hall, he'd been too drunk to grasp the importance of the location.

Whenever he went to other cities such as Edinburgh or Cardiff, their castles were always top of his places to visit, but because this had been there his entire life, he scarcely gave it a thought.

It wasn't tourism that brought him to the castle on a dull afternoon in March.

He pulled into the visitor's car park and paid the extortionate fees for an hour. Though it was dry when he got out of the car, a cutting wind came up the river from the North Sea. He fastened his jacket to the neck. He had no intention of paying the entry fee to enter the castle walls and bided his time at the entrance, getting a takeaway cup of tea to warm his hands.

His investigation had taken a surprising turn late last night when he'd been contacted by an old friend of Theo's. More than just a friend, Theo's ex. Roaul Bhatt had heard he'd been reaching out to Theo's acquaintances and had made the first move. Jason doubted he would have found Roaul on his own. Theo's social media profile were strictly Hart Stone business accounts, and he hadn't posted anything personal about his real life. Roaul hadn't featured anywhere. Roaul told Jason that the news of Dan Blumel's death had shocked him into coming forward.

Jason loitered around the entrance until two-thirty, when a man of Indian heritage walked out. He didn't know what Roaul looked like, but this man was around thirty and wearing the polo shirt and hoodie of the castle guides. This had to be him.

"Hi." Jason stepped towards him. "Roaul?"

The man nodded. His was very handsome in a wholesome, boy-next-door kind of way. Not at all like the sex-fantasy boys he'd seen in most of Theo's videos. He carried a lunch box and a Thermos flask.

Another nod. "We can go over there." He pointed to an empty picnic table on the other side of the car park. It was hardly picnicking weather, but Roaul said, "I've only got twenty-five minutes for lunch today, so I'll have to eat while we talk."

"Whatever is best for you," Jason said, falling into step beside him.

Roaul wasn't tall, five-seven at most. He knew Theo had been slightly built too and could easily picture them as a couple. They would have made an attractive pair.

"Thanks for getting in touch and meeting me," he said.

Roaul looked at him, before his eyes darted away. "I thought people had stopped caring about what happened to Theo."

"The police, maybe. Theo's family still care a lot."

Roaul seemed unconvinced. They sat and he poured a steaming cup of coffee from his flask. Jason took the lid off his tea and blew on the hot contents.

"I take it you never met his family?"

Roaul took a sandwich from his lunch box. It looked like tuna mayo. "No. He never met mine either. We were kind of in our own little bubble."

"How long were you together?" he spoke softly, not wanting to say anything that would freak Roaul out and cause him to clam up.

He chewed and swallowed. "Not long. About seven months. We finished a few weeks before he died. Though we were still in touch."

"Who ended the relationship?"

"I did. I knew what Theo did before we got together. I thought I could handle it. For a while I did. He treated what he did as a job. Was professional about it. When we were together, he was only ever focused on me. But as we got more serious about each other, I was the one with the problem. I couldn't separate who he was from what he did." He paused to take a sip of coffee before saying, "I was stupid."

"I think it must be a pretty normal reaction. Not many partners can be so open-minded."

"I wasn't open-minded. I was small minded. I worried what people would think of us. I was terrified my family would find out. They would never have understood."

Jason was touched by the melancholic sound of his voice. Roaul's deep regret was clear in every word.

"What was he like?"

"Theo?"

"Yes. I never met him. All I know about him is what I've seen online and what his brother has told me. I know very little about him as a person."

Roaul wiped his mouth on a napkin. The first glimmer of a smile appeared on his lips. "He was great. So full of life and enthusiastic about everything. He was a massive ball of energy. Supportive, too. He knew I was having trouble with my father. He was always there to listen when I needed him to be. Even after we broke up, I could still call him when I needed to talk something through."

It fit with the picture Jason was already beginning to form. The Theo he had seen online was a character, a self-creation. To a degree, he suspected that was also true of the brother Marc had known. There had to be something richer, something deeper about the boy behind Hart Stone.

"That must have made it hard to believe anyone could hurt him."

Roaul shook his head. "He had his share of haters. Most people who are successful at what they do attract negativity."

"What do you mean by haters?"

"Trolls. People would send him all kinds of shit. They would comment that he was ugly. That he must be riddled with STDs because of all the sex he had. They called him dirty because of the guys he let fuck him. It was nasty. Theo used to laugh it off, but I don't believe it didn't get to him. It must have hurt in some way."

"Did you ever witness anyone threatening him? Or was it all online?"

"Keyboard warriors. Those people who think they can say what they like from behind the screen of a blank profile."

"So, he didn't have any enemies you were aware of?"

Roaul finished the first half of his sandwich. "There was one guy who complained when Theo made more money from one of their collaborations than he did. I never understood the finer details of how it broke down. Sometimes they shared the production and editing costs of their film. Then they would each be able to post it on their own accounts. Other times, Theo footed the bill for the whole lot. Theo had way more fans than the other guys, so naturally he earned a lot more money."

"I don't suppose you remember the name of this collaborator?"

"His stage name is Trace Grey. I don't know what he's really called."

Oh, yes. Trace-get-to-fuck-Grey. Jason was still waiting to find out his real name so he could pay him a visit.

Roaul grimaced. "I'm not sure how he made any money. He was ugly inside and out but had a massive dick. I suppose that's all that matters to some people."

"Was Theo worried about this guy? Did he ever get physically threatening?"

"Not that I'm aware of. I don't think so. He's another one who talks big online but doesn't have the balls in real life." Roaul paused with the second sandwich, halfway to his mouth. His brow furrowed. "Oh, hang on. Trace…his real name is something like Tyrone. He used to work at The Viaduct." He grimaced. "I've no idea if he's still there."

Jason pulled out his notebook and scribbled the names. The Viaduct was Blyham's men only sex club. Why hadn't he thought of it before? If he was trying to track down sex workers, it was an obvious place to start. "Did Theo ever work there?"

"Not while he was with me. He didn't have to. He earned enough from the websites and occasional escort work."

Jason pricked up. "You knew about his escorting?"

Roaul chewed and nodded. He swallowed and sipped the coffee. "Theo was open about everything with me from the start. He said it was the only way our relationship could work, through honesty. I thought the same way in the beginning, but then it became too much for me to handle."

"Did he ever mention Soloman Archer?"

Roaul stiffened. "Theo was a professional. He respected client confidentiality. That's why they liked him so much."

"But he did mention him?" Jason pressed.

After a moment he replied. "Yes. I don't know anything else about him, though. It was a semi-regular thing. I don't think Soloman had much free time. Theo only mentioned him a couple of times while I was seeing him. They maybe got together every second or third month. It was a purely professional arrangement."

"Theo didn't say he was worried about Soloman? That he made him uncomfortable?"

"No. He was always in a good mood after one of their sessions. I think Soloman paid well and never asked him to do any of the kinky or degrading stuff some of his other clients were into."

It remained an avenue worth pursuing. He now had confirmation that Soloman used male escorting services. As a married, right-wing Tory, he had a lot to lose if that information was made public. His family, his career and reputation. Was that worth killing for? People had committed murder for a lot less.

Jason proceeded cautiously. "The night he died, Theo was outside the Vermont Hotel. Pretty fancy. Was he on his way to meet a client?"

"We weren't together anymore. I don't know." Roaul sighed and dropped the rest of his sandwich back into his lunch box. "I assumed so. He did meet guys there. He also filmed there a couple of times." He threw the dregs of his coffee away and screwed the cup back on the Thermos. "I have to get back to work."

"Just one more thing, please," Jason said. "You've been a massive help already. I'd like to speak to whoever filmed Theo's clips. It's very professional but he doesn't credit the photographers on any of his posts."

"I never knew him. He used to hire a guy from here in Blyham, but they fell out. After that, I think he used a photographer from Newcastle."

"What happened with the Blyham guy?"

"I really don't know the details. Theo said he made him uncomfortable."

"In what way?"

Roaul screwed his face up. "It's a struggle to remember all this."

"Please. Anything you can tell me will help."

"Don't hold me to this, because I could be confused. I might even be blurring more than one person. There was a photographer who shot most of Theo's stuff. They got on all right for a long time, but then this guy started making comments that Theo didn't like."

"Such as?"

"Telling him he was going too far. That he shouldn't do so much kinky stuff. He was working with too many interracial models. He thought Theo should go back to the vanilla boy-next-door stuff he started with. Theo hated being told what to do and he detested any kind of bigotry. He tolerated criticism of himself to a degree, but when this guy started dissing the diversity of his collaborators, Theo dropped him."

"Was there any fallout from that?"

"No. He found the guy in Newcastle and continued what he was doing. He never mentioned the other fella again."

Jason offered his hand and Roaul shook it.

"Thank you," Jason said. "You've given me some invaluable information."

Roaul smiled sadly. "I wish it wasn't necessary. I wish Theo was still here. Though we weren't together anymore, we were still great friends. Can you tell his brother how sorry I am. I saw the family at the funeral but didn't want to intrude. I...didn't even know what to say." He choked and turned his head away. "I had to watch from outside the cemetery."

Jason gently stroked his arm. "We'll do everything we can to get justice for Theo. I promise you that."

* * * *

Marc stood on the street looking at the office of Soloman Archer. He didn't know why he was there. What had compelled him to drive to this section of the city, just to look at a building? Soloman wasn't even in Blyham. Marc had checked his Parliamentary account, and he was in London for a vote that evening.

Marc had been unsettled for the last two days. So much had happened. The murder of Dan Blumel, giving his statement to the police, being confronted by Nadine in the carpark afterwards. That morning, he'd gone through the motions of work at the factory, but his heart and mind weren't in it. He had cancelled his diary appointments after lunch and got in the car for a drive to clear his head, but instead of heading for the coast, he'd found himself in the south end of Blyham.

Could Soloman Archer, a respected MP, really be responsible for the death of his brother and now Dan Blumel? It sounded so outrageous, and yet Marc couldn't get the idea out of his mind. It didn't matter how many times he told himself that he watched too much TV and real life was not a conspiracy thriller, he couldn't get past the theory.

There was nothing fancy about Soloman's office. It was nicely fronted in a good area of the city. It didn't scream high power and political corruption.

What the hell. You're here, anyway, might as well go inside.

The interior reminded him of a much fancier version of Jason's office. There was a large poster of the MP in the hallway. Marc studied the image. A bit like the premises, there was nothing wrong with the man. Fairly good-looking by most standards, a solid ten out ten compared to most other politicians. He was a blue-eyed silver fox who always looked a little uncomfortable in his fancy suits, like he couldn't wait to remove the jacket and roll his sleeves up.

Had Theo genuinely fancied him? Despite the big age difference, it was possible. Soloman was smooth-talking and handsome enough to convince the people of his constituency to vote for him, so no reason Theo wouldn't have fallen for him too. But was a boring, middle-aged bloke really Theo's type? The boy who loved a good time and to show off at every opportunity. It seemed unlikely. A business transaction then? Soloman was wealthy enough to pay whatever price for the services he required.

And murder?

Marc struggled to connect the dots that far.

He took a deep breath and went up the stairs.

There were two women in the reception area. He remembered what Jason had told him about them guarding their boss like lionesses.

The elder of the women sat at the desk. She was prim and efficient looking, in a sensible grey cardigan and huge glasses. The other woman looked like a former model turned political aide. Her honey blonde hair was salon blown. She wore sharply pressed grey trousers and a silk blouse which accentuated her athletic figure. Head to toe glamour.

"Hello," Ms Glamour-puss said. Her smile was dynamite, but her eyes were focused, taking him all in.

"Hi," he said. "I'd like to make an appoint to see Mr Archer when he's next available."

"Certainly. Trish, can you bring up the diary for the next surgery?"

The older woman screwed up her face and jabbed at her keyboard.

"My name is Marc Glass."

"Yes," said Glamour-puss. "I recognise you. Something of a celebrity in Blyham. There was no need for you to come into the office. You could have called and made an appointment. Mr Archer will be delighted to see you."

This was not the response he'd expected, given what Jason had told him about his efforts to get to the big man. "I was in the area," Marc said lightly. "Thought I might as well drop by."

"I'm delighted you did. It's a pleasure to meet you. My name is Chantelle. I'm Mr Archer's personal assistant." Her jolly tone seemed completely sincere.

Trish looked up from her screen. "The next surgery is fully booked, I'm afraid."

Chantelle tossed her hair and leaned over Trish's shoulder. "I'm sure we can do something. How does three-thirty sound? On the twentieth."

"Perfect."

Chantelle tapped the screen. "Reschedule that appointment for next month and put Mr Glass in there instead."

"Can I add a note about the purpose of the appointment?"

He watched them both closely. "I want to talk about the unsolved death of my brother. Theo Glass. He was killed by a hit-and-run driver last December."

Chantelle's cheerful smile turned to sympathy. "Yes, of course. That was a tragedy. Mr Soloman will be most interested in your concerns. And I'm truly sorry for your loss."

Marc didn't know what to say. A few days ago, Jason had been met with a hard wall of resistance when he came here. Now they were offering compassion. Something had altered and he wished he knew what it was.

Chapter Eleven

Night Life

"Something must have changed since I saw them," Jason said, shaking his head with a grin. "Do you think they spoke to Archer after my visit the other day and he's trying a fresh approach?"

"I have no idea," Marc said.

They were in the back room of The New Inn. Jason had suggested meeting there after work when Marc had called to tell him what had gone down at Archer's office. It was the first time they'd seen each other since Marc had left in the early hours, two days ago. Jason suspected it might have been awkward when they came face to face again and thought it would be easier over a drink.

"When I spoke to them, Chantelle claimed she'd never heard of Theo. Today, she's acting like your biggest fan and bending over backwards to keep you happy. That's a huge difference."

Marc seemed uncertain. "Maybe she has spoken to Soloman, and he reminded her of Theo's case. I was thinking on the way over here, if he cares anything about his constituents, he'd know all about the unsolved hit-and-run. He must have told her to be more accommodating the next time they heard from us."

"Nah. I left my contact details. If they'd made a mistake and wanted to be helpful, one of them could have got in touch. Instead, they waited until you made the next move. They're hiding something." Jason finished his pint of ale. It had only lasted a few minutes. Marc had barely touched his own drink. "I'll just get a top up and I'll fill you in on what I've found out."

As he waited at the bar, he glanced in Marc's direction. It was like the other night had never happened. That they hadn't slept together. Marc acted like they were a client and detective, just like before. It surprised Jason to find he was so wounded by the rejection. It was the right thing to do, he knew that. He'd crossed a professional line by having sex with Marc, and it could never happen again, but still, he couldn't pretend it hadn't happened.

He'd been thinking about it too much.

He hadn't even washed the bed sheets because he didn't want to lose Marc's scent from them.

Maybe when the case is over. For now, he had to focus on doing a good job.

He returned to the table. The place was filling up, but they still had a private corner to themselves.

"What's the big news then?" Marc asked.

Jason told him about Roaul Bhatt. "Did you know him?"

"No. I feel terrible that I don't. I don't know any of Theo's friends."

"He was at the funeral but didn't feel up to saying hello. He sends his best wishes." Jason told him about

Roaul's relationship with Theo. "They were together for six months or so, but even after they broke up, it sounds like they remained on good terms."

"Shit. I wish I'd known. Do you think he'll mind if I reach out to him?"

"Not at all. He contacted me, after all. He seems like a nice guy. But I got three very useful pieces of information from Roaul. The first—he confirmed that Theo was escorting for Soloman Archer. It wasn't a regular thing, but they got together more than once."

Marc's mouth dropped open. "Part of me hoped that Theo had been exaggerating when he told me that."

"No, it's true. Which makes Soloman's sudden willingness to talk even more suspicious, wouldn't you say. I think he's got no other motive than to find out how much you know."

Marc took a long, considered drink. "It's plausible."

"The other thing I discovered is that Theo had some kind of incident with one of the photographers he hired. Some guy he used on a regular basis overstepped the boundaries. He tried to tell Theo what to do. Dictate the kind of content he should be making and the guys he collaborated with. Exclusively white, by all accounts."

"Theo won't have liked that."

"According to Roaul, he didn't. He fired this guy, which makes him another person of interest. Unfortunately, Roaul didn't know his name, only that he's based in Blyham."

"Why didn't the police look into any of this?"

"They treated the case as a random hit-and-run. They didn't look any deeper."

Marc huffed and took another drink. "Do you think you can find him?"

Jason gave him a reassuring smile. "That's what you hired me for. Now, the third piece of information Roaul provided might make that easier than I thought. One of the models who frequently worked with Theo also had a disagreement with him over money. It doesn't sound too serious. Roaul couldn't tell me anything other than the model's professional name, Trace Grey. But I've had a friend of mine looking into that and he's come up with the guy's real name. Tyrone Lucas."

Marc leaned forward. "Have you spoken to him?"

"Not yet, but I'm hoping to. Roaul thinks this guy works at a club right here in Blyham. I'm going to visit the place later to see what I can find out."

"I'll come with you."

Jason raised his hands. "Whoa. Steady on. Remember what happened last time you insisted on doing that?"

"This is different. You just said it's a club. What could go wrong in a place like that? It's going to be full of people anyway."

Jason gritted his teeth. "Marc, this is not the kind of club you want to visit. Trust me. I can do this on my own and fill you in on what I find. I'll even call you when I come out, whatever the time."

Marc shook his head stubbornly. "No. I'll come with you. You can talk to him, I won't say anything. I just want to be there."

"Believe me you don't. Not in this place."

Marc sighed. "What are you taking about? What kind of club is it?"

Jason reached for his pint. "Don't tell me you've never heard of The Viaduct?"

* * * *

107

Marc went home first as Jason said they couldn't go to the club until much later. Jason had also warned him about the dress code.

"It changes most nights but, looking at their website, you could be asked to strip to your underpants. Wear something you don't mind being shown in public," Jason had said. Adding with a cheeky grin, "No washed-out old briefs."

Marc hadn't commented. He wasn't as naïve as Jason seemed to take him for. Anyone who was gay in the Blyham area knew about The Viaduct. Marc had never set foot in the place himself, but Theo had taken some delight in telling him all about it. Theo had been a regular at the club since he'd been old enough to get his hands on fake ID.

Marc hurried to put together an overnight bag and used a booking app to secure a room at the Vermont Hotel. This had every indication of being a late night and he didn't want to end it at Jason's flat again. The detective was incredibly attractive, but their priority had to be finding out what had happened to his brother. Jason didn't want to ruin things by falling for the man he'd hired to seek out the truth. They were lucky that they'd been able to write the other night off as a mistake and forget about it. *Forget about it? Hardly.* Marc doubted he would ever forget that, but they were mature enough to move on without fucking it all up.

He drove straight back to Byham and checked into the hotel. He'd reserved a decent sized executive room with a view of the river. It was Friday night, and the party crowds were already getting rowdy with stag and hen parties staggering between bars.

He showered and put on a pair of well-fitting black briefs with a white logo tastefully etched across the waistband. He doubted they would pass as sexy or sleazy enough for The Viaduct, but they were as far as he was prepared to go. He put on jeans and a crew-necked T-shirt. Again, Jason had warned him to wear something he could strip out of easily should the need arise.

Marc stopped himself from doing a search on the venue and finding out exactly how dodgy the place was and called for a cab instead to take him back to The New Inn where he'd arranged to meet Jason at ten o'clock. He got there twenty minutes early. Marc would normally have felt self-conscious going into a gay pub on his own, but the last few days had knocked down some of the walls he'd built around himself.

He hurried from the taxi, through the rain, and went straight in. It was a lot busier than when they'd been there earlier. The music was loud but hard to hear over the even louder voices of the crowd. He shook the water off his jacket and wiped his fingers through his hair at the door, noticing the appraising glances he received from several of the men around the bar. He hoped no one recognised him and tried to start a conversation. It had been a lot of years since he'd been on TV, but this mostly mature bunch were old enough to remember his era on *The Partnership*.

He ordered a glass of wine and waited close to the door so Jason would see him as soon as he arrived.

Marc felt hopelessly out of place. Was he too old for this? Going to bars on a Friday night? *Not really*. It had nothing to do with age. Rowdy night life had never appealed to him. Even when he was younger, he'd been too invested in work. He'd always had a job to get up early for most Saturdays. And even if there wasn't, he couldn't bear to waste a morning sleeping off a late night on the town. Jack had been the more sociable partner in their marriage. He was the one who had arranged to meet up with people, who booked all their holidays and made sure Marc had a life outside of work.

Marc had enjoyed it then, because it had made Jack happy. They hadn't spent a lot of time in the gay village. They weren't that kind of couple, but came to celebrate Pride most years and Jack had liked to have a big night in the city around his birthday. Without Jack, Marc found little reason to come out.

But without him, there was little reason to stay home either.

That house hadn't been the same since he died.

You're getting maudlin. Remember why you're here.

Theo had been the party boy of the family. He must have got a double share of the fun gene. He'd always known how to enjoy himself.

Marc glanced up as the door opened and was grateful to see Jason. The rain must have got worse in the time he'd been here—Jason's hair was soaking. He shook his shoulders to dislodge the excess water and wiped the back of his hand across his face.

Marc's heart beat faster.

Jason saw him and grinned. "Hell of a night we've picked for this." He was wearing a dark bomber jacket, fastened to the neck. "How come you're not soaked?"

"I got a taxi back here. Let me get you a drink to warm you up."

"I'll have a whisky, thanks."

Marc squeezed his way to the now-crowded bar and ordered another glass of wine for himself and a double for Jason. When he returned, Jason had removed his jacket. He wore a grey T-shirt. The damp had caused his nipples to stiffen, and they stood out proudly beneath the fabric.

Something else stiffened in Marc's pants too.

He passed him the drink. "I wondered whether you might have gone alone. You didn't seem keen on me coming along earlier."

"I'm not," Jason said, though there was nothing antagonistic in his tone. "I didn't think you wanted to blur the professional lines any further than we have."

Fair point. "I don't." The words sounded unconvincing, even to himself. Marc was already finding it difficult not to think about Jason's beautiful, uncut cock and wondering whether it was hard inside his pants. He remembered just how good it had felt inside him. *Focus.* "I just…want this to move along. I need answers. You sounded confident today that you would get them."

Jason shrugged. "It's difficult to know. This might turn out to be a waste of time for both of us." Then he grinned, displaying that sexy gap-toothed smile. "Though I'm grateful you're with me after all. When I left the apartment, I realised that I didn't fancy going to The Viaduct on my own."

"You've been before?"

He sipped the whisky and nodded. "A long time ago. When I first came back to Blyham, I had a few dates with a guy who was a regular. He talked me into going with him."

"How bad is it?"

"It's not bad, at all. It's just intense, and it's not really what I'm into. I don't judge anyone who enjoys it. Let's just say that I wouldn't choose to go there for any other reason than an investigation."

"The council keep trying to close it down, right?"

"They would if they could. But after the botched police work on the Blyham Strangler, they can't afford to piss off the gay community any more than they have. I've no doubt it will be back on the agenda soon enough. Once they think the dust has settled." He emptied his glass. "I really don't think it's your kind of place though. It shouldn't take me long to find our guy and speak to him. If you want to wait here, I could be back within an hour."

"No," Marc said, with more force than he intended. "I asked for this and want to come with you."

"Okay," Jason said, reaching for his coat. "We might as well get started." Then he put his hand on Marc's arm and added, "Don't say I didn't warn you."

Chapter Twelve

Darkness in The Viaduct

The man on the door at The Viaduct gave them wristbands, a drinks token and a clear plastic bag for their clothes. "You can undress in there," he said with a turn of the mouth that was part friendly, part lascivious.

Marc and Jason stepped through a doorway into a tiny changing area. It had a low ceiling and two wooden benches. The floors were bare. The maximum dress code for the night was underwear, but the two men in front of them who handed their clothes bag over to the attendant were naked apart from their shoes. One of them looked around twenty, with a slim, pale-skinned body and a flat arse. The other was stocky, fiftyish and balding. His cock was on the small side but when he turned around he had an attractively huge backside.

Jason gave Marc a gentle nudge. "It's not too late to go back and I'll catch up with you later."

Marc ignored the remark. He took off his jacket and pulled his T-shirt straight over his head. He might be naïve about the world of sex clubs and exhibitionism, but he was no prude. Besides, he exercised enough to keep himself in shape. Better than the average man his age. He wasn't about to go naked like those other men, but he wouldn't shirk away either.

"Okay, then." Jason took off his own jacket and sat to remove his shoes.

Marc stripped to his briefs and put his shoes back on. He was pleased with the underwear he'd chosen, they fit well and supported him in all the right places, but when Jason took off his jeans to reveal a black jockstrap with red piping around the groin, Marc suddenly felt very overdressed.

Jason stooped to stuff his clothes in the bag, giving Marc a pleasing view of his fulsome arse. *Fuck*. Marc's pulse raced again. No wonder Jason liked to wear jockstraps so much. With a butt like that, Marc would show it off as much as he could too. Jason straightened and caught him looking. Their gazes locked and held for a moment.

Marc swallowed and found his voice. "Ready?"

"Let's do it."

They checked in their clothes and headed into the main bar.

The Viaduct was situated in the cellars beneath Old Elvet Bridge. It was a network of vaulted rooms that had been used as warehouses before being turned into a club. Marc remembered reading an article from when it had first opened. The vaults had stood idle for decades, used only for tourist ghost walks, before they'd been repurposed ten or eleven years ago. There were three levels to the building, but as he walked into the ground floor bar, Marc struggled to imagine what must go on in the upper rooms.

Though it wasn't yet packed, he figured it would be soon. Low blue lighting illuminated a horde of bodies, most of whom had flouted the underwear code in favour of going fully naked. A lot of the men were on their own, though some pairings had already occurred on the edges of the room. The stocky guy who had arrived before them had already struck lucky with a younger black man who had the frame of a rugby player. He had his tongue down the throat of the older man and both of his hands clamped firmly on those wonderful buttocks. The men who had attained erections already made no attempt to conceal them. There were screens on the walls, playing porn, though no one paid them much attention. Why would they, with so much beautiful raw flesh all around?

Techno music blasted throughout.

Jason put his hand on Marc's waist. The touch sent sparks all through his body. Jason leaned into him. "You okay?" he had to talk straight into Marc's ear to be heard.

"I think so. Maybe we should get a drink and find this guy Tyrone." With so many men in here, he wondered how they would ever find anyone.

"Come on then."

Jason edged them towards the bar. Marc was glad that Jason didn't take his hand away from his waist until they were in position. The entry fee had included a drink. Jason took Marc's token and caught the eye of a bartender. He was a man in his late twenties, white, blond and heavily tattooed. Not Tyrone. Jason had shown Marc a screen shot of the man they were looking for before they arrived. He was younger, around twenty-four, with dark hair and a mean expression. The bartender wore a black G-string. Marc wondered at the hygiene of such an outfit when Jason asked him for two beers.

There was another man working the bar, but he was older. A heavy-set bear in backless trunks. He had a grizzly paw tattoo on his bare arse.

The bartender returned with the drinks. Before handing over the tokens, Jason leaned across the bar and yelled, "Is Tyrone working tonight?"

The bartender looked confused. "Who?"

"Tyrone Lucas."

"Never heard of him."

"I was told he works here."

The bartender turned down his mouth. "Maybe one of the other nights." He yelled something to the bear that Marc could not hear.

The bear finished the order he was serving and came over. Jason repeated the question.

The man's face was unimpressed. "Does he owe you money?"

"No. I just need to speak to him."

"He rip you off?"

Marc leaned nearer to hear what was said.

"It's nothing like that. I'm an investigator. I need to ask him about someone else. Tyrone's not in any trouble. I just need his help."

The man took in Jason's bare chest and smiled wickedly. "An investigator? Never seen one like you before."

"Well," Jason asked. "Does he work here?"

The man scratched his chin, giving it some thought. "Ah, fuck it," he said at last. He gestured to the hatch at the end of the bar. He stepped out where he could speak to them without shouting so much. "He might not be in trouble with you, but the boy is trouble himself."

"So, he does work here?"

"Not anymore. I fired him last month. I suspected he was thieving. A lot of the staff did. A bottle of beer here and there, I can turn a blind eye to that. And I'm sure that little bastard had his hand in the till. But one of the customers complained that he was hustling them for money. A couple more told me he was dealing on the premises. I can't have that. The council are looking for the slightest excuse to close us down. If we get done for dealing, then that's it. Licence cancelled. A scrawny little bastard like him doesn't give a fuck about the bigger picture. He just cares about himself."

As he spoke, Marc caught the way the man's eyes skimmed over Jason's body, checking him out. It was obvious that he fancied him. Jason seemed to notice too and leaned into him. "I don't suppose you could help me out and tell me where I could find him?"

"Give you his address, you mean? That would be another breach I could be shut down for. Sorry, handsome. You're hot, but not enough for me to break the law." He hesitated a moment, before reaching behind the counter and bringing out a mobile phone. He reached again for a note pad and pencil. "But fuck it, I owe that little shit nothing. I'll give you his phone number. You can call him and track him down from there. But don't tell him you're a detective, he'll block you. Let him think that there's something in it for him first. Then he'll speak to you. Money is the fastest way to that fucker's stony heart."

"What do you think?" Marc asked when they had moved away from the bar.

Jason folded the note with Tyrone's number on it and tucked it inside his shoe. "I think I want to speak to Tyrone even more now. The big guy's story tallies with what Roaul told me about Theo and Tyrone arguing over his fee."

"And the phone number?"

"Worth a call. He's already told me to get fucked on Messenger, but I might be able to appeal to his nicer instincts over the phone."

Marc rolled his eyes. The more he heard about this guy, the worse he became. A hustler, a thief and a drug dealer. Could he add killer to that list crimes? Was Tyrone the kind of person to steal a car and turn his brother down over their earnings? And to stab Dan Blumel at the gym in cold blood?

"You need to be more careful, whatever you do," he said to Jason. "This is getting shadier than I imagined."

Jason gave him a reassuring pat and swigged his beer. "I'm always careful. Except when I allow you to talk me into letting you tag along with me. When I finally track down Tyrone, *that* won't be happening."

As Jason tipped his head back to drink, Marc couldn't resist an illicit scan of his hairy chest and tight belly. That body was insane. In room full of naked men, Jason was hotter than any of them.

Marc took a swallow of his own drink. People continued to pour in the front door, though the bar didn't seem any busier than it was before. He was pleased to see a handful of other guys had kept their underpants on, so he didn't feel completely on his own about that. A few more wore jockstraps or backless briefs, but the majority of the customers were fully nude apart from their shoes.

"That's as much as we're going to learn from this place," Jason said. "Why don't we get dressed and call it a night?"

Marc hesitated and Jason picked up on it immediately.

"You want to stay?" Jason's lips twitched in amusement.

Marc was glad that the redness in his face would not show under the blue lights. "We've already paid the door charge and stripped off. It can't hurt to stay a while and find out what this place is really about."

"Okay."

"Theo was a regular here. I want to find out what he liked about the place...so I can understand him better."

"If you're sure."

"I am."

"I'll leave you to it then."

"No." The word came out too loud. Too panicked. "Stay with me, please. Just for ten minutes, while I look around. Then we can leave."

Jason's eyes twinkled in the artificial light. "Why don't we explore the place together?"

A narrow set of stone steps led to the first floor. Marc allowed Jason to show him the way. He watched his fine, hairy arse as he climbed in front of him. That jockstrap was such a simple thing, but it was outrageously sexual on a body like Jason's. Marc adjusted his hard on in his briefs, laying it along his hip to be less obvious.

The entire building smelled of damp. However thick the stone walls were, they held the clammy history of hundreds of years. He couldn't remember the exact age but was sure the bridge dated back to the late seventeen-hundreds. The builders who had toiled on its construction all that time ago couldn't have imagined what it would be used for now.

On the next level, the light changed from blue to red. Marc realised why it was not as busy downstairs as it should have been given the number of men who came through the door. He couldn't count how many there were in here, but the scent of their sweat, combined with poppers and sex, almost overpowered the dampness.

It took a few moments for his brain to catch up and make sense of what he was looking at. The main floor was one large play area. There were several slings, all of which were occupied by naked men getting their arses filled. The rattle of chains and the crack of flesh against flesh transcended the obligatory techno music. A man in his thirties with the honed body of an Olympic athlete was bent across a leather bench. His wrists and ankles were bound to all four legs of the bench. His muscles glistened with sweat as they took up the strain of the position. His arse was spread and open, his cock and balls had been pulled down to rest against the edge of the counter while a slightly built Asian man worked him over with his hand, alternating slaps between his butt cheeks and his genitals.

"Jesus," Marc gasped as he realised what was happening.

"I tried to warn you," Jason said in his ear. "This place is a lot."

He wasn't kidding.

The heat was intense. It had to be from all those bodies. Jason took Marc by the wrist and led him onwards. "You wanted to see what it was all about. Well, this is it."

A young blond man was laid out on some kind of vinyl-covered table, which spun like a lazy Susan turntable. His ankles rested on the shoulders of a muscle bear, who was giving it to his arse with long, well-controlled strokes. The boy's mouth was filled with the dick of a handsome Hispanic man. The man licked his lips in ecstasy. Marc could clearly see the bulge in the boy's throat with each inward thrust. And then both men pulled out of him and spun the turntable to swap his arsehole and mouth.

It was impossible not to think of Theo on that table. And as soon as the image was in his head, Marc wanted rid of it. He knew his brother would have revelled in every base pleasure The Viaduct had to offer, but he didn't have to like the idea.

Jason seemed to sense his discomfort and led him away.

His was aware of people watching them wherever they went and understood why. They might be in their thirties and forties, but for the men in here, they were fresh meat.

The heat and the smells intensified as they wandered deeper into the vaults. Jason guided him down a passage with a low ceiling. Along one wall was a series of small, separate arched rooms. Within each one was a plastic-covered booth. Every room was occupied by groups of two, three or four. He saw blow jobs, fucking, rimming, spanking. In one room a man lay on his back while another cleaned his feet with his tongue. The corridor was thronged with watchers and people waiting to take their turn.

At the end of the corridor stood a man, naked except for a black leather mask and boots. He had a well-built, powerful physique, but it was not his body that drew

Marc's attention, it was the mask. It was like a prop from a horror film. The soft leather mask covered his entire head and face. In place of the mouth was an open zipper. Sharp eyes peered from two narrow slits. They bore into Marc as they approached and caused a shudder. The man wet his lips and gripped his substantial cock at the base, causing veins to pop along its length.

If the effect was intended to be arousing, it had the opposite outcome. He was like a creature from a nightmare, an agent from hell.

Marc stopped and gripped Jason's wrist before they could go any further. Jason turned to him.

"Everything okay?" he mouthed.

"Let's go back," Marc said. Despite everything he had seen, the stranger in the mask had freaked him out the most.

In the main room, he saw the stairs that led to the next floor.

"What's up there?" he asked.

Jason drew level. His hand came around Marc's waist. "More of the same. Only it's darker up there. Pitch black in some areas."

Despite the heat, he shuddered. "I don't think I need to see that."

"No," said Jason. "I don't think so either. You ready to go?"

"I am."

As they headed for the stairs, he took a last look around. The slings were still in action. The athlete was getting his balls slapped on the bench and the blond boy was still turning on the lazy Susan. Marc struggled to make much sense of it. It was far removed from his own experiences of sex and the things that turned him on. There was a darkness here he did not understand.

He had to adjust his cock again as he followed Jason to the exit.

Despite everything, he was harder than ever.

Chapter Thirteen

"I Thought We Weren't Going to Do This Again."

Marc opened the mini-bar and extracted two small bottles of whisky. He held them up for Jason's inspection. "Will these do?"

"Better than nothing."

They were in Marc's hotel room. It had gone one o'clock. He'd had no intention of inviting Jason back, but after what he'd just experienced, all the things he'd seen at The Viaduct, he couldn't return alone. He would explode if he didn't have a chance to talk and debrief.

He took a bottle of water from the fridge to loosen the whisky if needed and put them on the coffee table. The executive room was a decent size. It was L-shaped, with the bedroom on one side and a sofa and sitting area around the corner.

He wondered if Theo had filmed in this room or entertained any of his clients and immediately shut down the idea. The lid had to go firmly back on that box for now.

Marc sat in the chair across from Jason and poured his whisky into a tumbler. He added the same amount of water. Jason took his neat.

"I tried to warn you not to go." Jason sat with one arm along the back of the sofa, his gaze fixed on Marc. Those large blue-green eyes were soft in the lamplight.

"I know. I take full responsibility for myself. And you were right. It was lot."

"You're thinking about your brother in there, aren't you?"

"I'm trying not to." He swallowed. "But yes. It's impossible not to. Is that what he was into? Group sex? Orgies?"

Jason crossed his knee over his ankle. It was raining again. Marc had left the curtains open, and it skittered down the window.

"Does it matter if he was? It's a shock at first. But I don't think it's a bad as you think. Everything that goes on in there is consensual. You heard the guy behind the bar. They need to keep everything above board. They can't risk losing their licence. What was going on looked kind of intense, but it was all harmless. No one really got hurt."

"Even the guy who got his balls smacked. That had to hurt."

"You know what I mean. He was doing what he wanted."

"And that guy with the mask? Shit, that was creepy. How can anyone find that a turn-on?"

Jason let out a soft chuckle. "All the colours of life and sex. Though I'll admit, the mask was scary. The guy under it was probably a pussy cat. A social worker or primary school teacher."

"Now, that is a scary thought."

"Look, I know it might not seem it, but that place has earned its place in the community. Last year and over the winter, when the Blyham Strangler was at large, The Viaduct offered a safe haven. Where guys could hook up without any fear they were taking a psycho home with them."

Marc hadn't thought about it that way. The murders committed by the so-called Blyham Strangler had been horrific, but he didn't have any first-hand experience of the fear and terror they had caused within the city. Marc didn't frequent the gay scene and rarely took strangers home for sex. His tame lifestyle hadn't made him a target for the crazed killer. Theo, on the other hand, would have been right in the thick of it. Living through every terrifying moment. *Jesus*.

He knocked off the drink and went back to the mini-bar. There was no whisky left. He pulled out a miniature vodka instead and poured it into his glass with a Diet Coke mixer.

"It wasn't a complete waste of time," Jason said. He finished his own drink and rose, picking up his jacket. "I've got some information to go on and will make a start on tracking Tyrone first thing in the morning."

"You're not leaving, are you?" Marc hadn't wanted to invite him back tonight, but the thought of him going caused a tightening across his chest. A mild panic.

Jason stood in the middle of the floor. His eyes were catlike in the low lighting. His magnificent body strained against his clothes. Marc remembered what he was wearing underneath.

"It's getting late. And I want to get started straight away tomorrow." His face was deadly serious. His gazed locked on Marc. "No time to lose."

Marc crossed the floor. Something possessed him. He flung his hand behind Jason's head and pulled him in for a kiss. Jason responded deeply at first, opening his mouth and slipping his tongue against Marc's, then he hesitated.

"I thought we agreed this isn't a good idea," Jason said.

It was the middle of the night and Marc had just been to a sex club, investigating his brother's death. He was a businessman, used to making good decisions based on sound evidence and judgement, but right now he couldn't tell a great idea from a disastrous one. All he knew was that he wanted Jason.

He pressed his hips against him, revealing the full extent of his arousal, and sought his mouth to continue the kiss. Jason's reluctance disappeared and their mouths opened in passion. Marc's head was light, and it had nothing to do with the alcohol. He wrapped his arms around Jason's torso, his hands searched the muscular planes and ridges of his back. Jason's own arousal was evident as they ground their bodies together.

"Let me see your jockstrap," Marc murmured.

Jason licked his lips. "You liked that, did you?"

He nodded. "Do you wear them often?"

Jason grinned, then drew his tongue along Marc's jaw, all the way to his ear, before he whispered, "Just when I'm feeling hot."

Marc's cock throbbed harder. It seemed impossible to be turned on any more than he already was, but Jason kept making him harder and harder.

They broke apart and Jason unfastened his jeans, shoving them to midthigh. His cock strained against the black material of his jock. Marc had never really considered their erotic appeal before. They'd always been something he thought of as practical, a piece of sportswear. But on Jason's body, they were fit for a far different kind of physical activity.

Jason gripped the bottom of his T-shirt and raised it to show the jockstrap in full. Then he turned around, giving Marc a clear view of his rear. His big, meaty butt was perfectly framed by the black and red straps. He transferred his weight from side to side, flexing his cheeks.

Marc's dick swelled even harder. He moved close, sliding his palms across Jason's arse to take a buttock in each hand. He squeezed, savouring the weight and density of his flesh. He pressed his face to Jason's neck, rubbing the skin, before kissing and tasting the mild saltiness of sweat.

"Your arse is amazing."

Jason chuckled and pushed back against his hands. He turned his head to seek Marc's mouth and they kissed again. It was all intoxicating. The heat, smell, contact of his body. The scent of shampoo in his hair, the tobacco notes in his cologne, the detergent on his clothes. Everything about him was arousing.

Marc wanted to go much further than he had the last time. He guided Jason towards the bed and pushed him face down on top of it. Before Jason could react, he fell on top of him and buried his face in his arse. Jason gasped in surprise as Marc parted his cheeks, seeking out his opening.

"Is this all right?" Marc asked.

"Yeah. I'm totally vers. Knock yourself out."

He savoured all of it. The damp sweat in his crevice, the soft brown hair that coated the lower halves of his cheeks. The hairs in his crack had been trimmed to keep his beautiful, dusky pink opening clear. Jason shuddered when Marc drew his tongue across the smooth skin of his hole and the skin of his arse rippled with gooseflesh. Marc went to work with fervour, teasing Jason with the tip of his tongue, taking delight as he squirmed and pressed his hips into the bed.

"That's amazing," Jason whispered.

Marc hadn't eaten a man's arse since Jack. His late husband had adored it, and Marc was able to take him to fresh heights of pleasure every time. He'd never imagined he'd want to do this to another man again, but there was something about Jason that drew him in and made him want to relax the barriers he'd put up around himself in the last few years. Marc had never believed he would enjoy this level of intimacy again.

His emotions were in chaos. One minute he was determined he would never have sex with Jason again, and the next he had his face planted in his arse and was tonguing his hole like it was the only thing in his life that mattered. Grief worked in the strangest of ways. Grief for his husband, grief for his brother, it had coloured his life for years.

But Jason was alive and so was he. After the stress of the last few days, they deserved to indulge their deepest desires again. Right now, Marc was nothing but an animal. A creature of instinct. And his instinct was to continue.

"Let's take off our clothes," Marc said, pushing back from the bed.

They undressed hurriedly. Marc stripped all the way but was quietly pleased when Jason removed everything but the jockstrap. With a wickedly sexy grin, Jason leapt back on the bed and arranged himself on all fours. His back was arched, and he presented his butt to Marc.

"It's all yours," he said. Gazing at Marc over his shoulder, he planted a hand on his right buttock and spread his cheeks. His dark hole glistened with saliva.

Marc raced to the bathroom to retrieve a condom and a bottle of lube. He was from an era when safe sex really mattered and always came prepared. He tore into the packet, never taking his eyes off Jason's arse as he unrolled the rubber down his hard dick. The last time Jason had fucked him, it was what they'd needed at the time. Now their roles were reversed, and he wanted to experience Jason from the other perspective. He lubed his cock, then applied more to Jason's hole, pressing into him to prepare the way.

"Is this still all right?" he asked, as Jason's tight passage gripped his fingers.

"Fuck me," Jason demanded, holding himself strong on his hands and knees. "I want you inside me."

Marc swiped his cock up and down the crease, teasing his hole for a moment, before angling to the opening and pushing in. The tightness of his body was instant ecstasy. Marc told hold of Jason's hips and leaned into him, until his pelvis pressed against Jason's butt. The view from above was stunning. Jason's broad back, his compact waist and prime beef arse — now filled with Marc's cock.

They took a moment to adjust to each other.

The rain rattled heavier against the window.

Marc moved inside him, gently, until Jason demanded more. "Really fuck me. Like the way those guys were getting fucked at the club."

As his mind flashed back to the hardcore sex he'd seen all around in The Viaduct, Marc gave him what he wanted, pulling back until just the tip remained inside, before thrusting into the depths. He gave it to him with long, steady strokes, increasing in speed and force. The sounds of their skin smacking together obliterated the rain. Jason's wide back glistened with sweat. Marc ran a hand across his spine, placed it on his shoulder and fucked him even harder. They gasped and grunted together, engrossed in each other, lost in sex.

"Fuck me," Jason growled through gritted teeth.

Their breath came faster and more ragged. There was no way to prolong this. They were too caught up in the raw, animal passion of their fuck to hold back.

The catch in Marc's desperate grunts signalled the end. He cried out, helpless, as something inside him tightened, his balls throbbed, the insides spasming in the most intense and pleasurable way.

"Oh, God," he cried. It was almost too much. The spasms continued all through his groin, building, intensifying, getting stronger, prolonging the exquisite ache as he came. With a roar he buried his cock inside Jason and surrendered to the orgasm as it rode right through him.

Jason let out a deep-throated laugh as they moved apart. He turned to reveal the wet front of his jockstrap. "I didn't even touch myself," he gasped. "I just shot my load spontaneously. I'm pretty sure that's a first."

It had been a night of many firsts for both of them.

Marc went to the bathroom to dispose of the condom. When he returned, Jason had removed his damp jock and lay naked on top of the bed. He gazed at Marc with soulful eyes. "You don't mind me lying here, do you? Or are you going to chuck me out?"

Marc laughed and flopped face down onto the bed beside him. "No chucking out from me."

Jason rolled onto his side. He ran his hand along the curve of Marc's back. "That's progress then. I thought we weren't going to do this again."

Marc murmured, turning his head to face him. "Neither did I. It doesn't seem like such a big deal anymore."

"Tonight upset you? Going to The Viaduct?"

"Upset is the wrong word. It's just... I don't know. Opened my mind. Made me think about Theo in a different way."

"Just because he went to the club, we have no idea what he used to do in there. And like I said earlier, during the Blyham Strangler days, a lot of guys went there. It was the safest place to go for sex."

"I'm not judging him for what he used to do. He lived a far more enlightened life than I ever have."

They lay quietly for a while, lost in their own thoughts and listening to the incessant rain.

"I wonder if he was there tonight?" Marc said at last.

"Who?"

"Whoever killed my brother."

"What makes you think that?"

"I don't know. It just came into my head."

Jason's hand lingered in the small of Marc's back. He said, "If it was anything to do with Soloman Archer, then I very much doubt it. The reason Soloman hires escorts like Theo is because he can't be seen with other men in public."

"I guess you're right. I know you say it's a safe place, but to me, it just felt dangerous."

"It's different, not dangerous. Unlike the other bars across the city, I'm not aware of a single incident of violence being reported in The Viaduct. For Blyham, that's remarkable."

Marc sighed then yawned. "I'm knackered," he admitted.

"You should sleep. Forget all about this until tomorrow."

The warmth of Jason's hand on his back was comforting. "Will you stay?"

Jason moved closer. "If you want me to."

"I do."

They got up and slipped beneath the covers. Marc turned his back so Jason could spoon in behind. Despite the turmoil and confusion in his mind, Marc fell asleep within minutes.

Chapter Fourteen

The Hustler

Tyrone Lucas answered the door in a pair of grubby grey sweatpants which hung low enough to expose his hip bones. Jason knew from his videos that Tyrone was shorter than the models he had worked with, but he was not prepared to tower over him so much. The pasty skin, dark hair and sharp features were as expected, but Tyrone was a lot more rodent-like in person and his skin was in poor condition, with black shadows beneath his eyes, broken veins around his nose and across his cheeks and dry, broken lips. The overpowering pong of cannabis wafted from the apartment.

"Hi," Jason said, holding forth his ID.

Tyrone sucked his teeth and leaned against the door frame. "Have you got the money?"

Jason gave him two twenties and a ten. "Half," he said. "You'll get the rest after we've talked."

Contempt flowed from the younger man in waves, then with a tut, he snatched the cash and opened the door wider. Jason stepped inside. Tyrone's sweatpants drooped from his flat backside, exposing a good two inches of butt crack.

The bedsit was tiny, with a kitchen area in one corner and a tattered sofa pulled close to a TV and gaming console. The surfaces were littered with dirty dishes and mugs, pizza and takeaway cartons, empty bottles and full ashtrays. The whole place stunk of weed, body odour and damp.

Jason was more surprised at the other side of the room. The bed and surrounding space were immaculate, with crisp white sheets and freshly painted walls. There was a phone on a tripod facing the bed and a bright selfie circle light. A second, traditional video camera stood on a tripod at a different angle. It was obviously where the magic happened.

Jason noticed the lights were switched on.

"Are you filming?" he asked.

"About to," Tyrone said, scratching his crotch. His famously huge dick waggled in his pants. "Till you turned up."

"On your own?"

"What does it look like, mate? Unless you wanna bend over and take it, there's no other fucker here." He gave his cock a squeeze to emphasise the point.

"I'll pass on that. This won't take long if you tell me what I want to know."

Tyrone grimaced, then stepped over a pile of dirty plates to drop onto the sofa. Jason wondered whether Tyrone's subscribers had any idea of what was on the other side of the camera. It would destroy any erotic delusion.

Jason was about to take a seat but thought better of it when a mouse scurried across the floor to disappear beneath an upturned pizza box.

Tyrone retrieved a half-smoked joint from an ashtray and lit it. "Come on. Time is fucking money. What do you want to know?"

"I want to know about Theo Glass. You might have known him as Hart Stone."

Tyrone held the smoke deep in his lungs and exhaled slowly, deliberately taking his time. Testing Jason. He didn't respond.

"I know who the fucker was. I don't know what you expect me to tell you, other than he was a thieving cunt."

"You didn't like him?"

"Couldn't have given half a shit about him either way. He was the one who contacted me after seeing my content. He said we could make a video together. I didn't fancy him, but that doesn't matter when there's money involved. I've fucked a lot worse."

"Did he make all the arrangements?"

"He booked that poncy hotel, if that's what you mean."

"Which hotel was it?"

"The Vermont." He took another hit on the joint.

Jason had suspected as much. It put a tragic taint on the incredible time he had spent with Marc there last night.

"What else?"

Tyrone could not keep the irritation from his tight face. "Like what?"

Jason pointed at the tripods beside his bed. "You didn't film on those. I've seen the footage. It was professionally done."

He sucked his teeth again and nodded. "Theo arranged all that too. Phone cameras weren't good enough for him. He had to have a pro."

"And what, you shared the costs?"

"Fuck no. He wanted the fancy photographer and professional edit. He paid for it. Waste of fucking money. People who want to see a big cock, they don't give a shit what it was filmed on. They just want to see it, you know what I mean." He tugged his pride and joy to make his point. "I don't need any of that shit when I've got this. Theo, though, what did he have? Below average dick and a slack hole. He needed all that fancy equipment to make him look good."

"You said he ripped you off. Did you agree to split the profits fifty-fifty? Even though he funded the shoot."

"We agreed we could both use the clips on our own sites. Only he made a fuck load more money from it 'cause he had more subscribers. But don't you think I should have been entitled to a big cut of that too, seeing it was my dick his fans were paying to watch him ride?"

Jason decided not to stoke Tyrone's sense of entitlement and ignored the question. "Did you ask him for half of his subscription fees?"

"Not half. No. Just for the first month our clip went live. That's what everyone was watching and that's what I deserved a cut of."

"Didn't your own site see an upsurge in subscriptions too?"

"Not like his," he sneered. "And before you fucking ask, no I didn't run the stupid bastard down 'cause I was pissed off about the money he owed. I was angry, but not that fucking angry."

"What about Dan Blumel? You did another scene with Theo. A three-way with Dan."

He grimaced, showing small, brown teeth. "We did."

"Was that before or after the scene with Theo?"

"Same fucking day, mate. Don't you know how this stuff works? We shot the scene with me and Theo in the afternoon, then Dan comes by about five o'clock and we did the threesome. That hotel costs a fortune, Theo wanted to get his money's worth. I think he did a solo dildo scene before checking out the next day."

"Theo sounds like a shrewd businessman."

"Con man, more like."

"Did Dan have any issues with Theo? Did he feel ripped off too?"

"Doubt it. They shot a load more scenes together."

"Did you get on better with Dan? Were you friends?"

"Fuck no. I couldn't stand him. But I've already told you, you don't need to like someone when there's money involved." He sucked the joint dry and tossed it in the ashtray. "Speaking of which. Do I get the rest of my money now?"

Jason laughed. As unpleasant as Tyrone was, he couldn't help admiring his single-track agenda. "It seems to me that you didn't know Theo that well at all. What can you tell me about the guy who did the filming?" He'd already heard from Roaul that Theo had issues with one of his regular photographers. He was interested to know if that was the man Tyrone had worked with.

"He was full of his own importance as well. You'd think he was shooting a multi-million-pound series for Netflix rather than a cheap gay porno. I don't know what Theo paid him though."

"Does he have a name?"

Tyrone gave an exasperated sigh and rolled his head. "Blake something. Remar, I think. I'm not sure. I didn't have anything to do with him, other than take his bloody directions. He was always bitching about the light, or a hand that was in the wrong place and blocking his shot. I don't think he liked me but I'm not doing this to make friends. I don't need to waste money on a poncy photographer when I've got this." He groped his cock again.

He's obsessed with that thing.

"How did Blake treat Theo and Dan, was he the same with them?"

"He didn't like Dan, for obvious reasons."

"Which are?"

Tyrone scoffed. "'Cause he was black. Blake treated Theo like a princess. He made no secret of the fact he thought Theo was slumming it with a black man."

"So, he's racist?"

Tyrone shrugged. "It was more than that. He thought Theo had dropped his standards to get fucked by poor white trash like me too. Racist, snob, dickhead. Call him what you like."

"How did Theo react to that?"

"He was pissed off, but he was more concerned about getting a return on his investment. He tried to keep everyone sweet on the day, but it was obvious he didn't like the way Blake treated Dan and me."

Tyrone jumped up from the sofa. He's sweatpants had slipped even further, exposing the base of his cock. He jiggled impatiently from side to side. Jason was losing him.

"One last thing. Do you think Blake was in love with Theo, or a bit obsessed with him?"

"Obsessed for sure. He acted like the sun shone out of his arse. Might as well, that bloke had everything else stuffed up there at one time or another." He gave a high-pitched, stoned laugh.

"Enough to hurt him?"

"You mean to run him down? I've no idea. I doubt he had it in him. Probably just went home and kept wanking over Theo's old clips. The ones without black guys or white trash partners, obviously."

Jason took fifty pounds from his wallet and handed them over. "Thank you, Tyrone. I appreciate your help."

He took the money. "Any idea who did it yet?"

"I'm still working on it."

"Probably just some arsehole who'd taken too much coke or had too much to drink. Theo wasn't the type to make enemies, you know. He was too basic."

"Did he ever mention escort work to you?"

"No. But If you keep asking questions, I'm going to need another fifty."

Jason smiled and headed for the door. "Good luck with the rest of your work." He jerked a thumb towards the bed.

"You know, if you ever fancy making some content, I'd be up for it," Tyrone said.

Jason paused, at a loss for what to say.

"You look all right," Tyrone continued, giving his cock a tug. "And it's quite a popular scene, you know. Older, beefy guy, getting topped by a small, skinny dude. Users like that."

Jason opened the door. "Thanks for the offer, but I'll stick to my day job."

"If you ever change your mind, you've got my fucking number."

* * * *

Jason returned to the office. Ryman was in with a client and Olivia finished early on Friday afternoons. He made a mug of tea and started straight in on tracing Blake Remar. It took less than a minute to find his website. Tyrone had done well to deliver his real name. There was no mention of adult content on Blake's corporate-looking site, just lots of business photographs, high-end food pics and arty wedding shots. Filming sex workers was obviously a side hustle.

Unless Tyrone had been messing with him and had given the random name of any photographer he knew. Jason's instincts were that the boy was telling the truth. Beneath the swagger and the bad attitude, he'd come across as genuine. Almost endearing, despite it all. Though Jason wouldn't be taking up the offer to get fucked by his enormous dick on camera.

He chuckled.

There was one photograph of Blake on his bio page. It was very slick and processed, making it impossible to get an idea of the real man. He could be anything from twenty-five to fifty. His face was whited out by a combination of lighting and filters. He was blond, possibly good-looking, with what appeared to be blue eyes. There was no trace of personality, or even humanity in the image. His smile was fixed and lifeless.

Jason reached for the phone.

He expected to reach a secretary or receptionist and was surprised when the answer came, "Hello, Blake Remar."

"Oh, hello. This is Blake I'm speaking to?"

"It sure is." The voice dripped with oily charm. "How can I help you?"

"Hello, Mr Remar. My name is Jason Durham, I'm a private investigator."

"Investigator?" The voice faltered on the single word.

"I work for the brother of Theo Glass. I understand you had a working relationship."

There was a long pause before he replied. "I…did a favour for Theo and photographed him once or twice. I hardly knew him, though. I'm not sure how I can help."

"I know about the adult content creation. I understand you shot quite a few of Theo's videos."

"I don't know where you've got this information from." There was no charm in the voice now, just pure hostility.

"From more than one source, Mr Remar. I'm not looking to do you any disservice. I'm trying to get a picture of Theo's life in the months leading up to this death. I'm contacting as many of his acquaintances as I can."

"I ceased working with him long before he died. I don't see how I can help you."

"Do you remember when you saw him last?"

Blake sighed. "I don't know. Sometime last summer."

"On a shoot?"

"If that's what you want to call it, yes. Theo booked a hotel, and I went along to film him and some of his… friends."

"You'd worked together a few times before that?"

"Yes."

"I've seen some of the stuff you did together. Very professional. It seemed like you had a good collaboration going. Why did you stop working together?"

Jason heard Blake take a deep breath. "Look, I started filming him as a favour. It's not the kind of work

I usually do. I didn't want to continue and that was the end of it."

"A favour? So, you must have known Theo pretty well. You must have been good friends to get involved in something so risqué."

"I've told you all I know. I did him a favour a handful of times then stopped. That was the end of it. I didn't see him for months before his accident. I have nothing more to add."

Blake hung up.

Wow. Aggressive. Defensive.

Blake Remar knew more about Theo than he was prepared to acknowledge.

Jason took out his notebook and drew a circle around his name. Blake had just become his prime person of interest.

Chapter Fifteen

A Grieving City

If Marc had ever been to Julie's Bar before, he had no memory of it. Either that or the place had changed considerably. Though not as old-fashioned as The New Inn, it was a traditional pub with a friendly atmosphere. He'd arranged to meet Jason here at seven for a drink before they went to get something to eat. He'd kept the room on at The Vermont for another night and had got a surprising amount of work done there today without the usual distractions of being in an office. Marc had finished everything he needed to by five. He'd done a quick workout in the hotel gym, showered and changed, and arrived at the pub twenty minutes ahead of time.

The video jukebox was playing Kylie Minogue when he arrived. The place was reasonably busy, but from the way they were dressed he guessed these were people having a drink after work, rather than those at the start of a night out.

Just a week ago, Marc would have felt out of place coming into any of the bars in the gay village by himself. How much had changed since he'd instigated the investigation and met Jason. This world, which had seemed so alien and unwelcoming to him before, was almost a comfort now. By discovering the venues on the scene, even The Viaduct, he felt like he was getting to know Theo in a way he'd never been able to when he was alive.

He could imagine his brother in here. Surrounded by friends, having a laugh and making the most of life.

With a sudden stab to the heart that had become all too frequent, Marc was flooded with regret for the things he'd never said and now never would.

There were two women working the bar. One with white and blue hair approached him with a smile and took his order. He went for a medium glass of white wine. As she fixed the drink and took payment, he noticed a framed photo on the back wall of a handsome man around forty years old. There was a plaque beside his picture. *In loving memory of Phil Logan,* it read.

Of course. Phil had been one of the last victims of the Blyham Strangler. Because he had been a stranger to the LTBTQIA community, Marc was only beginning to realise the devastating effect the murders had had on the people here. He gazed at Phil's picture and another wave of sadness washed through him. Such a tragic waste of another young life.

Then he started to see all the community posters and notifications that adorned the walls around the pub. Helplines, support meetings, crisis centres. Free personal alarms were available for anyone who needed them. Though the Blyham Strangler had been captured, his legacy of violence would haunt the city for a long time.

And now there had been another death. Dan Blumel's name could be added to the catalogue of tragedy.

Marc took his drink and found a table. It was on the inside but close enough to the wide doors of the heated beer garden. The outdoor area was well covered and there were a lot of people taking advantage of it.

Jack would have loved it here.

If his husband had been alive at the time of the Strangler murders, he would have been galvanised to take action himself. Jack had been far more community minded than Marc ever was. When they were younger, Marc had focused all his energy on making his business a success, while Jack had always been more people focused. If it hadn't been for Jack, Marc would never have taken time for holidays or leisure pursuits.

Had Marc wasted the time they'd had together? He'd spent so long in the office when he could have been with his husband, making memories. They'd had no idea how short their life together would be.

Nobody did.

Would Theo have done things differently too, if he'd known what little future he had? Or Dan Blumel? Or any of the other young men who had lost their lives in this vibrant community?

The memorial behind the bar had triggered something. It was unfair that his brother's life should be forgotten. And what was he doing now, if not trying to cover up Theo's lifestyle? To stop it from coming to the attention of their parents. When Nadine Smythe had approached him with her intention to investigate Theo's death, Marc's initial reaction had been panic. Fear that his mother would discover the truth.

Would she even be shocked? Theo was her baby, but she couldn't be so naïve to think he was an angel. Had Theo even made much of an effort to conceal what he did? He'd been proud of his adult content creation when he'd talked to Marc. Had he also confided in their mother? Marc had never asked. He'd been too scared to face the facts.

Shit. What the hell am I doing?

He was coming at this from the wrong direction. Hiring Jason to discover the truth about Theo before Nadine could expose it, when what they should really focus on was finding out who killed him and celebrating his life.

Marc sighed wearily and tasted the wine.

Not bad.

An exceptionally handsome couple came into the bar. They both had dark-brown hair. The younger of the two, in his mid to late twenties, was tall with large eyes and a strong jawline. The older partner looked to be in his late thirties. He was very serious-looking with startlingly pale grey eyes. They held hands. From their body language, and the way they moved together, they were so obviously in love.

When she spotted them, the bartender who had served him hurried out from behind the bar and rushed over to them. She embraced the younger man first, hugging him tight. It was a display of touching and raw affection. She wrapped her arms around the older man more carefully.

"Is this okay?" she asked.

"I'm fine," he replied. "Really. It doesn't hurt much at all now." His accent sounded French.

Another song started on the jukebox and Marc couldn't hear what else they said. The woman returned to her position behind the bar and served their drinks.

Jason came through the door a moment later. His face was serious as he scanned the room, until he spotted Marc and broke into that staggeringly sexy smile. He had come direct from work, and still managed to look incredible in chinos, a navy jersey and bomber jacket. He walked straight over to Marc.

"Hey, I didn't expect you to be here already."

Marc's melancholia evaporated with his arrival. "I walked from the hotel. I had no idea how long it would take."

"You should have got a cab up. This city still isn't the safest place to be walking the streets." Noticing Marc's puzzled expression, he continued, "A fella was queer bashed earlier in the week on Broad Street. The Strangler might have been caught, but there's still a lot of people about who hate us."

"Noted."

"Can I get you something?" Jason gestured to the bar.

Marc shook his head. "I've barely touched this. Just see to yourself."

When Jason went off for his drink, Marc couldn't resist checking him out. His beefy butt filled the seat of his pants. Until last night, Marc had fought against his attraction to Jason. Now he didn't want to resist. So what if they were breaching professional boundaries. They owed it to themselves to seize a few moments of happiness when they were presented.

Jason returned with a pint of bitter. He took off his jacket and hung it over the rear of the chair. His nipples were hard, poking against the material of his jersey.

"Good day?" Marc asked.

Jason sipped his pint and nodded. He licked the foam off his top lip. "I found Tyrone and tracked down Theo's photographer."

Marc straightened. "You did? How?"

"I just called the number we got from The Viaduct for Tyrone."

"He agreed to speak to you?"

"For a hundred quid."

"Huh. And what did he say?"

"Apart from offering to fuck me in one of his videos, quite a lot. He was rude and offensive, but I think it was all an act. Underneath, he was just a kid who's had to look after himself for a long time. He's getting by the only way he knows how."

Jason filled him in on what had occurred at Tyrone's flat.

"Does he really think Theo was a conman?" Marc asked.

"Nah. He's just pissed off because Theo had more subscribers than he did and therefore was making a lot more money. As he should have, Theo paid for everything relating to the shoot. He did Tyrone a favour by letting him share the clip fifty-fifty."

Marc sighed. He still hadn't watched any of Theo's adult content. He doubted he ever would. As much as he wanted to learn more about his brother and understand his life, he didn't need to see that.

"And the photographer?"

"Very cagey. He didn't want to talk to me at all. He tried to play down that he had even worked with Theo."

"Does that make him a suspect? Was he so possessive of Theo he would have hurt him? It sounds like a stretch."

"It makes him a person of interest. And it ties in with what Roaul told me. He's now at the top of my list for further investigation."

"I wonder if we'll ever know what happened?"

Jason reached across the table and put his hand over Marc's. "Every day we're learning something new and getting closer to the truth. We'll find out eventually."

The pub began to fill up around them. The after-work crowd moved on and were replaced by the genuine evening punters. The good-looking couple who had arrived earlier carried their drinks from the bar into the beer garden, where they joined a small group of people who were as happy to see them as the bartender had been. There were hugs and tears all around.

"Do you know who they are?" Marc asked quietly.

The French man sat down, and a pretty black woman put an arm around his shoulder, while wiping away a tear.

"They're the guys who caught the Blyham Strangler," Jason spoke in a hushed tone. "The older guy, Mallon, he was stabbed in the process. The younger one is called Roman. They were his intended victims."

Marc had heard details of the case on the local radio while driving, but he'd never read any of the news articles.

"No wonder they are getting heroes' welcomes," he said.

"They're lucky to be alive. Even luckier to have each other."

Marc felt a lump in his throat as watched them, then turned away. He knew what it was like to be stared at and be the centre of ghoulish attention. Those men deserved their privacy. Despite being heroes, he recognised the cloud of grief that hung over the men and their friends.

"Shall we go for food soon? I'm starving." He'd been so caught up with work at the hotel, his lunch had consisted of a cup of tea and a small packet of complimentary biscuits.

Jason nodded. "Me too. Though we might struggle to get in anywhere on a Friday night."

"Where do you suggest?"

"Well, if you appreciate good-quality food, without the fancy frills of a posh restaurant, Chez Michelle is always good. It's up in the city centre. About a five-minute walk."

Marc laughed. "You think I'm a snob, don't you?"

Jason feigned shock. "I never said that."

"You didn't have to. I get the message. And FYI, Chez Michelle is actually one of my favourites."

Jason winked and knocked off his drink. He stood and hauled his jacket on. "Let's go."

It was a relief to step outside and find that it was not raining. This must have been the first day in weeks when it hadn't poured, but there was a cold bite to the evening wind. Marc fastened his jacket to the neck. He was already looking forward to a hot meal, and hopefully afterwards, some hot action with Jason if he was up for it.

They put their hands in their pockets and crossed to the other side of the road.

"We can cut along Broad Street, past The New Inn, then up towards the centre," Jason said.

"Didn't you say it was unwise to walk around like this?"

"We should be okay. There are two of us and it's still early."

Marc exhaled. "It's sad, isn't it? That it should come to this. People afraid to walk about at night."

"It is. In the last weeks before they caught the Strangler, these streets were crawling with police. Despite the continued hate crimes, they disappeared once they'd caught their Big Bad."

They were deep in conversation and not paying attention to their surroundings when Marc's senses suddenly prickled.

In the next second he heard the roar of a car engine.

He spun around to catch sight of blinding headlights rushing towards them.

He grabbed Jason and pulled him aside as the car mounted the kerb, coming straight at them along the pavement.

He caught a quick glimpse of a black car and darkened windows.

Then the vehicle struck. They were both tossed over the bonnet and the roof of the speeding car.

Chapter Sixteen

A Rush of Death

Jason realised what was about to happen a second before impact and prepared for the hit. He leapt into the air, avoiding the full force of the bumper, spinning across the window and roof before landing with a roll on the other side of the vehicle.

There was no time to stay down. Ignoring the pain in his shoulder and right side, he pushed into a crouch, and saw the fiery brake lights as the car came to a stop about fifty yards ahead, still up on the pavement.

Marc was behind him, face down on the ground.

There was a harsh grinding of gears then the scream of the engine as the driver put the car into reverse.

Marc was out of it. There was no way Jason could lift him in the time they had.

Jason fell on top of him, heedless of his weight. He wrapped his arms around Marc and hauled, twisting and rolling. His body was a dead weight, but Jason summoned the strength from somewhere. He spun over him, pulling with all he had, gaining momentum to send them sprawling over the kerb and into the road.

There was a screaming blur of black metal and red lights as the car ran over the spot where they had lain seconds before. The driver mustn't have seen their roll to safety.

Before the maniac could react further, Jason got up and heaved Marc across his shoulder. No longer thinking, he allowed his survival instincts to take over.

The car reached another screeching halt. The pavement was streaked with skid marks. The air filled with the stench of burning rubber.

He heard another noisy gear change as the car was shoved back into first. The driver was coming for them again in a rush of death.

Hoisting Marc into a firefighter's lift, Jason ran in front of the approaching car. The weight on his back was immense. Pain shot up his legs from an injured ankle. He didn't have the speed he needed.

He wasn't going to make it.

Then he crashed into the recessed doorway of a warehouse.

The slipstream of the car tore across his back as it sped by them.

There was the further screeching of brakes, followed by the blare of car horns. Other vehicles had arrived, skidding to a stop as their drivers realised what was happening.

Jason eased Marc into a sitting position, sheltered by the doorway.

The car that had tried to run them down was at a standstill on the pavement ahead of him.

It was a black saloon. He struggled to focus on the registration plate.

Who the fuck was in there?

Suddenly Jason was consumed by rage. He reacted with instinct again, racing forward, pounding the pavement towards the car. When he caught whoever was inside, he would beat the shit out of them.

Getting closer, he made out the first couple of letters on the plate, NC.

The engine gave another roar and the vehicle lurched forward. There was a crunching sound as the chassis tore against the kerb when it crashed down from the pavement to the road. Then, with an eruption of speed, the car sped to the end of the street and shot around the corner.

Jason staggered to a stop. The pain in his ankle and ribs increased a hundredfold.

There were voices behind him. Shouts for help.

He turned to see someone leaning over Marc in the doorway. A woman nearby on her phone.

The reality of what had just happened landed heavily and his legs gave out from under him. Jason collapsed to the ground, unable to take another step. His voice was capable of only one word.

"*Marc.*"

* * * *

"Where is he?" Jason asked. Just the effort of talking caused his head to hurt, as if a spear had been driven through his skull. The bright lights of the hospital treatment room made him wince. He shielded his eyes with his hand.

Jason had just been wheeled back from the X-ray department. He'd been fortunate, according to the radiologist. He had one broken rib on his right side.

Other than that, he'd walked away from the impact of the car with a mild concussion and a sprained ankle.

The British Asian nurse who'd been in charge of his care since he'd been admitted urged him to be calm. Her name was Melony. "Don't get agitated," she told him in hushed tones. "You're going to be discharged soon. You need to relax as much as possible."

"But where is Marc. Where is he?"

"Your friend went into surgery while you were having the X-rays."

"Surgery!" *Shit*. He'd known Marc had taken the brunt of the impact, but no one would tell him how serious his injuries were.

"Don't worry," Nurse Melony said, as she wrapped a blood pressure cuff around his left arm. "He'll be fine. He'd didn't get off quite as lightly as you did, but he's doing well. He has a broken arm. The ulna on his left side. He needs surgery to reset the bone before they put a cast on."

He breathed with relief and closed his eyes against the light. It was painfully bright. "Is that all?"

"He's concussed, like you are. And he'll be sore all over for a few days, but he's been lucky. You both have."

Lucky. Some crazed idiot had driven a car onto the pavement and tried to run them over.

Just like Theo.

Coincidence? At the same time as they were investigating Theo's murder. *Not fucking likely*.

They were getting closer to the truth. Maybe too close.

The blood pressure cuff inflated, squeezing his arm.

"You don't happen to know your friend's next of kin?" Melody asked. "He said he didn't want anyone notified of his accident, but there must be someone who wants to know."

His parents. Poor Marc. He wouldn't want them to know the exact same thing that took the life of their youngest son had almost befallen him. Everything they were doing was for their protection.

"I don't know," he said. Only half true. He could have found their contact details easily enough. "But it's late. There's no point worrying anyone until the morning. Especially when you say he's going to be okay, right?"

"I guess not. But if he was my brother, I'd want to know."

She finished his blood pressure check and pronounced him in good condition. "The doctor will be along in a few minutes to discharge you."

"I want to wait for Marc."

She nodded. "I'll find out which ward they have taken him to and let you know." She put away her equipment. "There's a police officer outside, if you want to talk to him."

He nodded, then winced at the pain the movement triggered. "Send them in."

He was a grateful a moment later when a familiar face stepped through the curtain. Benito Coppola. The Detective Sergeant was his usual smart, handsome self. Even in the middle of the night, he managed to turn it out.

Jason had already given a detailed statement straight after the crash.

"Any news?" he asked.

Benito stood over him. His head and broad shoulders blocked out some of the horrendous florescent light. "Last week I met you at the scene of one murder. Now tonight, I'm here because someone tried to kill you. Are you ready to tell me what's really going on?"

Jason ignored the question. "Did you find the driver?"

"Not yet. But we found the car. It was burned out on the coastal road. Remind you of anything?" Benito pulled out a chair and sat beside the bed.

Jason shielded his eyes against the glare again.

"Marc hired me to investigate the murder of his brother."

"I figured that out for myself."

"What about the car?"

"Stolen. Like the one that killed Theo Glass."

"Someone doesn't want us to know the truth."

"Maybe someone should have trusted what they were doing to the police." Was there a hint of animosity in Benito's voice? Jason definitely detected a note of sarcasm.

"Because the cops did such a great job with the initial investigation," Jason shot back defiantly.

Benito rolled his eyes. "Fair point. And Dan Blumel?"

"He was going to tell me what he knew about Theo on the night he was killed."

"Fuck. Why didn't you tell us any of this?"

Jason massaged his forehead. "Lower your voice, will you? It fucking hurts."

Benito edged closer but spoke softly. "Come on, if you are on to something, you have a duty to share it."

"How come the police didn't know this stuff anyway? I don't have your resources or manpower, but I tracked Dan down in no time."

"And you almost got yourself killed. You have to stop and let us take care of it from here."

Jason shuffled up the bed. He tried to sit forward until the pain in his broken rib gave him an excruciating reminder to keep still. "Are you people going to put any more effort into tracing the driver who came after us tonight, than whoever killed Theo Glass?"

Benito pursed his lips and nodded. "After tonight, they'll have to."

Jason gazed at the detective. Benito was genuine. He wanted to truly believe that Blyham police would treat the case more seriously now. Maybe they would, for a day or so at least, maybe until the end of the week. How much faith could he put in Benito, anyway? Just because he was gay it didn't mean he was an ally to the community. As a Detective Sergeant, he was embedded in the institutionally homophobic Blyham force.

"How's the investigation going into Dan's murder? Any suspects? Any arrests?"

"I'm not on that team."

"Of course you're not. And yet we both know the answer to those questions is no." Jason sighed and put his forearm over his eyes again. The light sensitivity was crippling. The doctor he'd spoke to earlier had told him it could last up to forty-eight hours. "Just leave me alone. I've told you all I can for tonight. All I care about right now is knowing Marc is okay."

"I need to know what you've discovered about Theo's death," Benito said insistently.

"Then get a fucking warrant. Marc is my client, not Blyham police. I'm already doing your damn job for you. If you want to know who is responsible for this, put some genuine fucking manpower into the investigation instead of your bullshit lip service."

Chapter Seventeen

Recovery

On Sunday it rained again.

Marc sat on the sofa in the living room of Jason's apartment, gazing absent-mindedly at the water that streaked the glass of the balcony door. His left arm, encased in plaster from hand to elbow, was propped up on a cushion on the arm of the sofa. Jason had pulled the coffee table closer so he could elevate his feet too.

Marc had been discharged from hospital that morning and hadn't wanted to go home. He hadn't told his family about what happened on Friday evening and wanted a place to lie low for a couple of days until he felt better. He would go see them on Monday or Tuesday when he'd had a chance to think of how best to break the news. To tell them what he'd been doing, about Theo's lifestyle and how he had almost succumbed to the same fate beneath the wheels of a maniac driver.

It was shitty of him to keep them in the dark, but he needed to process it himself, before he dealt with anyone else's reaction.

Jason was in the bedroom, on the phone to his business partner Ryman. Jason had also managed to keep the details of their near-death encounter to himself so far, but owed it to Ryman to fill him in. Marc hoped Ryman went easy on him. Jason had been through enough already.

He'd tried to take care of Marc, fussing around when he'd arrived at the apartment that morning, but Jason needed time to recover himself. He was in pain. Marc caught the way his mouth pinched, or brow tightened, whenever he tried to stand, or put too much weight on his sprained ankle.

Despite everything, they had been lucky. They were still alive to continue the investigation. To find the bastard responsible for Theo's death.

The bedroom door opened, and Jason limped into the living room. He held a hand across his injured ribs. The shadows beneath his eyes were deep.

"How did it go?" Marc asked.

Jason gripped the back of the armchair for support. "He's glad we're both okay, but oh boy, is he pissed."

"You could have been killed."

"He knows that. But he also knows I broke the golden rule. Never get into a relationship with a client."

"It's too late to change that now."

"It doesn't stop him being mad about it."

"He can't fire you. You're full partners, right?"

Jason gave a weary sigh. "He wants to take over your case. He says I can't continue when I have a personal interest in the investigation."

Marc shuffled to the edge of the sofa and rose carefully. "I'm the client. I'm paying for the case. I want you, not Ryman."

"He'll have calmed down by tomorrow. He's just shocked to find out about us. I have no intention of stepping aside, but it might not be a bad idea for him to join us. We're getting closer. We could use his help."

Marc moved in behind him. He put a light hand on Jason's waist, careful not to hurt him. Though it was only his rib that was broken, Jason was bruised all over. Marc hadn't seen the full extent yet, but the bruises that showed on his arms and neck were severe enough. He leaned close and brushed his lips across his ear.

"Is that a good idea? We could be putting him in danger too," he asked.

"The sooner we catch this bastard, the sooner we put an end to it."

Marc nodded and rested his chin on Jason's shoulder. He was right, but whoever was responsible might become more desperate and more dangerous the closer they came to the truth.

"Come and sit down," Marc said. "You haven't stopped since I got here."

"I'm too wired."

"You need to rest to get better," Marc insisted. "Sit and I'll make you some tea."

"Hey, you're the invalid, remember. I'll make you tea."

"No, you won't, sit. I've got a broken arm, which doesn't make me an invalid. Besides, I'm right-handed."

Jason reluctantly agreed and took a place on the sofa. Marc got familiar with the layout of the kitchen and found the teabags and mugs. He put the kettle on to boil.

"What are we going to do next?" he asked.

Jason put a cushion on the coffee table and carefully lifted his sprained ankle onto it, grimacing as he did it. "For the rest of today, we do nothing. But first thing tomorrow, I'll pick up where we left off, and find out all I can about this photographer guy, Blake Remar. Well, almost first thing. Ryman wants to see me in the office to tear me a new arsehole first."

They both laughed, then Jason clutched his rib.

"Ouch. Laughing is a bad idea," he said. "Don't make me do it."

Marc made the tea and carried it over, one mug at time, before joining Jason on the sofa.

"This is nice," he said, shuffling closer to Jason. "Just a quiet afternoon together. It's like something real people would do."

"Real people probably do it without the injuries and concerns about a murder investigation."

"Probably," Marc said lightly. "But this is still nice."

"Mmm," Jason agreed.

They relaxed into each other's company. The tea, together with the strong painkillers Marc had been prescribed, left him in a chilled mood. They chatted about things other than what had been happening. Jason told him about his earlier life and his career in the Navy. Marc wanted to see some photos of him in uniform, but they were both too comfortable and mellow to get up and seek them from the other room.

"I bet you looked handsome in the Naval gear," Marc said.

"You know, you could be right."

Then they laughed some more, and Jason complained about the pain in his ribs again. Jason turned on the TV and they spent a lazy hour channel hoping, dipping in and out of a variety of brainless afternoon shows. Marc dozed off for a while. The aftereffects of the anaesthetic he'd had for his surgery had left him groggy and tired. When he woke, sometime around four, Jason was swearing at the television.

"What's up?" Marc asked, blinking to regain focus. He hated this fuzzy feeling. He rarely slept more than a few hours a night. Falling asleep through the day was something he only ever did at Christmas. There was a clip from a political chat show playing. He recognised it as a regular Sunday morning programme. The news channel was showing highlights of that day's edition.

"This prick," Jason said. "Man of the fucking moment."

It took Marc another second to realise who was on screen. It was Soloman Archer. Marc sat up straight, suddenly alert.

Soloman was being interviewed by the main presenter. He wore a grey three-piece suit, a candy-pink shirt and a lurid pink and blue tie. He spoke with the oily confidence of a politician.

"What I hear on the doorsteps, is that people have had enough of this woke gender ideology. There are far too many children around today who think it's fine to self-identify as God knows what."

The clip ended and cut back to the news studio.

"What was all that about?" Marc said. The pain in his arm made it difficult for him to get comfortable.

"As if he wasn't insufferable enough, he's stirring up transphobia for the sake of looking tough. 'What I hear on the doorstep.' Absolute bullshit. He wouldn't lower himself to go knocking on doors in Blyham. And if he did, he wouldn't hear any of that rubbish. People are more concerned about the cost of living, and whether they can feed their kids or afford to put fucking petrol in their tanks this week. They're not interested in his culture war."

"Why is he coming out with this anyway?"

"'Cause he's a fucking clown."

Marc stroked Jason's thigh with his good hand. "Hey, you need to keep calm, remember."

"I was calm until that shit-merchant came on TV."

It seemed strange that Soloman would want to raise the issue of trans rights and gender identification, given the skeletons he had concealed in his own closet. Was the man so arrogant, he believed he was untouchable?

Probably. He was an MP for the nasty party after all.

"What else did he have to say?" Marc asked.

"Nothing worth hearing. Bastard! I can't wait until we get the evidence we need to nail him."

"Do you think he's behind it all?"

"He's the most likely suspect."

Marc was not so sure. Soloman had plenty to hide, not least his relationship with Theo and however many other sex workers he used, but would he really go so far as murder to keep his secret?

"It can't have been him on Friday night."

"I know," Jason said. "I've already checked. He was in London all day. But it doesn't mean he didn't hire someone to do it."

"They can't be any good if he did. We're both still here."

"We were lucky. Theo and Dan can't claim the same."

When Marc stood up, his entire body ached. It was too early for another dose of painkillers. "Do you mind if I take a bath? It might help."

"Go ahead. You know where everything is."

Marc slowly made his way to the bathroom and set the tub running. He was glad he'd kept himself in such good physical shape before the accident. If he hadn't, his recovery could have been a lot worse.

With Jason's help, he wrapped a plastic bag around his plaster and undressed.

"Jesus," Jason said as Marc's shirt came off. His torso was mottled with purple and black bruising.

"I'm trying not to look at those," Marc said. "I don't imagine you're in any better condition."

"It seems much worse seeing the damage to someone else. *Shit*. We really could have been killed."

"That was the intention."

He got the water to a comfortable temperature and, with Jason's hand for support, he eased himself in, before topping up the hot. He sat back, enjoying the warmth while keeping his plastered arm over the side. Jason perched on the edge of the bath, looking down at him. There was a soft smile on his face.

"What is it?" Marc asked.

"You're the first person besides me to use that tub. It's nice, that's all. Having you here."

Marc felt a warm surge, inside as well as out. "It's a pity the circumstances weren't better than this."

"Agreed. If they were, I'd be sliding in there with you."

"Let's keep that thought as something to look forward to."

"It's a promise." Jason ran his fingers across Marc's knee where it rose above the water. "Want me to bring you anything?"

"I'd love a drink. A nice cold glass of wine."

Jason chuckled. "Nice try. But you know booze is off the menu for the next few days. For both of us."

"Spoilsport."

"What about dinner? There's no way either of us are cooking, but I can place an order. It will be here by the time you get out."

"I like the sound of that. How about pizza? We can have it straight from the box. No washing up."

"Even better." Jason leaned over to give him a kiss on the lips and left him alone.

Just a few days ago, this would have seemed impossible, spending a lazy Sunday at Jason's place, relaxing on the sofa, soaking in his bathtub. How rapidly everything had changed. *Is that what happens after a near-death experience?* Priorities change beyond recognition.

Meeting Jason and making a connection with him were the best things to come out of this ominous situation.

Marc sank deeper into the water, until it covered his shoulders, allowing the heat to ease the ache in his muscles.

The calm was broken after a few minutes.

Jason bolted back into the room. His phone was ringing.

"It's Tyrone."

Marc pushed back into a sitting position.

Jason answered the phone and put it on speaker. "Hello."

The deep base of grime music came over the speaker. The line was terrible, like the caller was driving. "That you?" a voice demanded.

Jason shrugged his shoulders at Marc. "It's Jason Durham. Who are you expecting?"

The next words were incomprehensible, then, "...got something more to tell you."

"What is it?"

"Gonna cost you. A lot more than last time."

"And this is something you've just remembered?" Jason's voice dripped with sarcasm. "What has jogged your memory?"

"Hearing you was nearly turned into roadkill, mate. That's what. It's not fucking happening to me. I want three grand so I can get out of Blyham."

"What is it you've got to offer that you couldn't before?"

"Stop dicking me around. I know what happened to Theo. That's what you want to know, ain't it?"

"I don't believe you. I don't trust you."

"Believe me or not, but it'll save your life. Three thousand quid. Cash. Let me know when you've got it and I'll tell you where to meet."

The line went dead before Jason could say another word.

Chapter Eighteen

Danger by the River

"We can put him off until this evening," Jason said, pulling on his shoes. He winced. It hurt like hell to bend down. He hitched his foot onto his knee to tie the laces. "Once I finish work. I'll been done soon after five."

Unexpectedly, he had a full day in the office ahead of him. Ryman had demanded a meeting for ten o'clock which would likely run until noon, then he had booked him in for a full afternoon of appointments. In between all of that, he wanted to find out all that he could about the photographer Blake Remar.

"I don't want to wait that long." Marc slipped his arm, bulky with a plaster cast, into a sling. "I'll find out what he knows and fill you in afterwards."

Tyrone's call last night had left them on edge. Jason had no doubt Tyrone knew more about Theo than he'd revealed so far but doubted whether he'd be forthcoming with all the information. He'd give them a little bit, then come back in a few more days with a higher price.

"He's a grifter. I know what he's like, just let me handle him. I'll make it clear this is the last penny he's going to see."

Marc sat on the end of the bed beside him. "This might shock you, but I've been a successful businessman for over twenty years. I know how to strike a deal and I can smell a bullshit artist from a mile away. I'll pay Tyrone what he's asking for today, but that's in exchange for everything he knows, nothing less."

Jason put a hand on his leg. "All I'm saying is this kid's a shark. Your broken arm will be like blood in the water to him. He'll sense weakness and exploit it."

"Then he's in for a big surprise, isn't he."

He could see there was no point in arguing any more. He understood Marc's urgency to move on with the investigation, but there was already a target on his back. Whoever had come after them on Friday would likely try again. "Let me see if I can rearrange my appointments. I'll come with you."

"Ryman is already pissed off with you. He'll go ballistic if you start neglecting your other duties. And I'd feel exactly the same in his position. Go to work, do your job and we'll catch up later."

"What if Tyrone was the driver on Friday? This could be a trap."

"Do you think he is?"

Jason sighed. "In all honesty, no. He's a thief, and a conman, but I doubt he's violent. Physically, you could hold him down, even with a broken arm."

"There you go then. Nothing to worry about. I'll get him the cash, find out what he has to say, and tell you all about it tonight."

Jason didn't like any of it, but Marc would not be discouraged.

"Call me as soon as you get there. I want to be in on the meeting."

"You mean if anything goes wrong I'll have a witness."

"Just do it. Please."

Marc put his hand on top of Jason's. "I promise."

* * * *

The stairs to the first-floor office were trickier than Jason had predicted. After two days of rest, his sprained ankle didn't feel any better and neither did his broken rib. The painkillers he'd taken with breakfast did little more than take the edge off. He gritted his teeth and gasped until he reached the top.

Ryman was waiting. The stern, angry face he'd prepared for Jason's arrival, dropped at the sight of him.

"Shit, you look awful," he said as Jason reached the reception desk.

Olivia jumped up from her chair and hurried to him. "My God, you do. You shouldn't even be here, you should still be in bed."

"She's right," Ryman said. They crowded around him. "I'm taking you straight home."

"Guys, just back off, will you. Give me space. I don't want to go home or go to bed. I'm here and I want to get on with things, okay. Don't make a fuss."

Undeterred, Olivia unbuttoned the top of his shirt and peeked down at his chest. She gasped on sight of his bruises and beckoned for Ryman to take a look.

"You're black and blue all over," she said.

"It's worse than it looks." A lie, but if he said it enough times he could almost believe it was true.

They continued to make a fuss. Olivia plied him with tea and biscuits, until he went through to Ryman's office for their meeting.

The anger Ryman had been filled with yesterday seemed to have dissipated now they were face to face. He watched as Jason uncomfortably shrugged off his jacket and sat. "I really don't think you should be here."

"I want to be here," Jason said. "I want to be doing something. If it gets too much, I'll go home early, but right now, let's just get on with things." He was in half a mind to ask Olivia to cancel his afternoon appointments so he could go with Marc to see Tyrone, but Marc had already made his feelings clear. Work had to come first.

"I think you'd better start at the beginning," Ryman said. "Tell me everything that's been going on with this case."

Jason did as he asked. He skipped over their visit to The Viaduct, but otherwise left nothing out. He told him everything about his relationship with Marc and how it had developed.

"You can't continue with his case under the circumstances," Ryman said.

"I know, and I'm not," Jason said. "This isn't a case anymore. Someone tried to kill me as well as Marc. It's personal. I need to find out who is behind this before they try again. I'm no longer acting for the business. This is for me and Marc."

Ryman nodded in agreement. "I think that's for the best. But that doesn't mean the firm won't be involved. I want to see everything you've got and I'm going to help you. The sooner this mess is resolved, the better."

"You don't have to do that. You've got your own workload."

"But I've only got one partner," Ryman said. "An attack on you is an attack on all of us."

A ball of emotion welled in Jason's throat. He swallowed with difficulty. "Thank you."

"What about Soloman Archer? Do you think our fuck-wit MP has anything to do with this?"

"My guts tell me yes. But I haven't found any evidence against him. I haven't even been able to speak to the fucker yet. He's been in London the whole time."

"That counts for nothing. I'll start digging deeper into him. Find out what else he's involved with. Any dodgy connections. Dubious partnerships. The bloke is worth a fortune and few people build that kind of wealth by playing nice."

"I can't work him out at all. And he's got so much to lose. Fair enough, he likes to screw around with young guys on the side. I dare say he's not the only member of Parliament who gets up to that. But Theo wasn't exactly discreet about their arrangement. Why take the risk?"

"It gives Soloman more reason to silence him, though. Theo was blabbing his mouth, so he had to shut him up."

Jason scratched his chin. "I know, that's the obvious conclusion, right. But why do it in such a high-profile way? Wouldn't a fake overdose drawn less attention? Or a stage robbery that goes wrong."

"You're making the assumption that he has access to the kind of people who can arrange those things. And was prepared to pay the price tag that comes with a professional hit. The way Theo was killed and the botched attack on you, doesn't say professional to me. It smacks of local lowlifes doing it for a few hundred."

"But again, why? He's much more likely to be caught out that way. You know what the local criminals are like. They would sing like a canary if they were arrested in connection to the attacks."

"It won't hurt to ask some questions." Ryman had a string of contacts in Blyham's criminal community. "People are talking about what happened to you on Friday night. There must be some rumours about. I'll find out what the word is. What else have you got?"

"I need to follow up on what Tyrone told me about this photographer. There was some kind of disagreement between him and Theo. It will probably amount to nothing, but I'd like to speak to him anyway and find out what he knows."

Ryman nodded. "Fair enough. You get onto that, and I'll start making some calls. Let's see what we can dig up."

Jason exhaled with relief. "You don't have to do this, but thanks."

Ryman got up and came around the desk. He sat on the edge, looking down at him with the face of a kind uncle. "I can't lie, this time yesterday I was furious about what you've done. But I can see the bigger picture. Some bastard came after you and we need to find them before they try it again."

* * * *

Marc stopped at a high street coffee shop after visiting the bank. His entire body ached, especially his back. He'd underestimated how tough the recovery process could be on the body. He ordered a tea and a chocolate brownie, hoping the sugar boost would revive him. He eased himself into a chair by the window, with a view of the railway station. While he waited for the tea to brew, he dialled Tyrone's number.

"Who's this?" Tyrone snapped.

"It's Marc Glass. I'm Theo's brother. I'm the one who hired Jason and I've got the money you asked for."

"Er, where is Jason?" The angry tone had shifted to one of suspicion. He had a very strong, regional accent.

"He's working. I've got the cash you want so you can tell me what you know."

"Money first. Then I'll talk."

It was no less than he'd expected. "I'm in the city centre right now. I can meet you whenever. Just tell me where you are?"

A long pause, then, "After what happened to the pair of you, I don't want you coming by my place. You can keep your trouble to yourself."

"I already told you, I can meet you anywhere."

"All right. I'm seeing a client at two. You know the footpath that runs along the river, downwards from the concert hall?"

"No, but I can find it."

"Just walk down from the hall, it's about five minutes along the river."

"Why don't we just meet inside the hall?"

"Cause I don't wanna be fucking seen with you in public, that's why? Don't wanna become Blyham's next piece of roadkill, do I? I'll be there at four, or thereabouts."

Tyrone hung up before Marc could respond.

Jason hadn't been kidding about the kid's attitude. It stunk. He wondered how well Theo had known him. Though Theo hadn't been hung up on things like class.

It wouldn't have bothered him how rough or unmannered Tyrone was. Besides, they'd been collaborators, rather than friends.

Marc poured the tea and settled back in his chair. He had a few hours to kill before he met Tyrone. He wasted time on his phone, searching for news reports on their hit-and-run. There was nothing online that he didn't already know. The car that had hit them was a Mercedes E-class saloon. It had been stolen from a side street in the west of the city earlier that afternoon and had been found burned out soon after the incident. Thankfully, neither he nor Jason had been named as victims in any of the reports.

Marc's parents were still unaware of what had taken place. It pained him to hold back from them, but it would only cause so much worry. They had been through enough. If he could keep it from them until they made a breakthrough in the investigation, it could only be for the better. It wouldn't just be the attack he would have to tell them about. The entire story of Theo and his lifestyle would have to be revealed and he wasn't prepared for that conversation yet.

He spent an hour going through his work emails and making phone calls. His heart wasn't in the job, but it gave him a distraction from everything else. Afterwards, he moved on to another café further along the street, where he ordered lunch and did some further research into Soloman Archer, reading up on his backstory and voting history in Parliament.

It made for grim reading. Soloman was as far right as it was possible to go. Anti-European, anti-union, anti-migrant. He'd voted against several progressive LGBTQ and trans policies. He also had his fingers in private health companies with an interest in dismantling the NHS.

What a piece of shit. Marc doubted whether his brother would have been aware of any of this, or if he would even have cared. Theo had never shown any interest in politics or national issues. He rarely had anything to say about current affairs or news. The only reason he would have even known Soloman was an MP was if Soloman had told him. Soloman would have been a source of finance and little else to him.

And what had Theo been to Soloman? A disposable piece of arse? An inconvenience? A liability?

Marc took his next dose of painkillers and got an Uber to take him from the city centre to the concert hall. This was as far as the vehicle could get to the river side footpath. He would have to walk the rest of the way. It was a cold, gloomy afternoon, but there had been no rain for several hours and he hoped it would stay that way.

Fastening his jacket to the neck, his shoved his good hand in his pocket and set off along the trail. The exposed fingers beneath the plaster cast immediately felt the chill but he had no way of warming them. Maybe he would be able to convince Tyrone to come back to the warmth of the concert hall once he'd gained his trust. *If I gain his trust.*

Marc had been aware of this footpath but couldn't recall walking along it before. It was a lot nicer than he'd expected and he was sure he would have remembered it. With the wide river Bly on one side and a well-established park on the other, it was lined with trees, cycling lanes and a children's play area. The Vermont Hotel was directly opposite on the other side of the river.

Marc consulted the tourist direction sign. According to the map, the footpath followed the course of the river all the way to the North Sea, six miles down. Tyrone hadn't told him exactly where to meet. Surely, he couldn't mean that far.

After a few minutes, Marc reached a park bench and paused. It was five to four. He checked the path in either direction. There was no one else in sight. He keyed a quick message to Tyrone, telling him where he was.

There was a splash in the river ahead of him. A quick flick of a fish tail on the surface before it darted away. Something sizeable by the disturbance it caused.

For the first time, Marc doubted the wisdom of coming alone here, especially with three thousand pounds of cash in his pocket.

Four o'clock came and went with no sign of Tyrone.

Jason had shown him photos of the young man, so he knew who to expect. He checked his phone again. There was no reply to his message.

The cold quickly intensified as a chill wind came off the water.

By ten past four he was still waiting. Marc shivered. He couldn't stay here for much longer. He decided to give Tyrone until quarter past. If he failed to show by then, he would go to his apartment with Jason once he had finished work.

As the sky darkened, the path took on an ominous aspect. The trees were bare of leaves. Spring had yet to stake a claim on the long, cold winter. In another month, this same area would look very different. He imagined it thronged with dog walkers and joggers, but on this bleak afternoon in March, it had a sad, haunted quality.

He waited five minutes beyond the cut-off he'd already decided upon. His fingers and toes were numb. He couldn't wait here any longer. Tyrone was a no-show. Marc decided he would head for the warmth of the concert hall café and let Tryone know he could find him there until six o'clock. The kid was likely messing him around. Fucking with him for some twisted reason. Though Jason was adamant Tyrone was all about money. Why would he set up an exchange with no intention of collecting? Even if he made up a pack of lies about Theo — which in all likelihood was what he'd do — he would still expect payment for it.

Fuck it.

Marc started walking back along the river and pulled out his phone. He dialled Tyrone's number.

Jason is right. The kid is a grifter. No doubt the price would go up the next time they spoke to him.

He got the dial tone.

Marc froze, half a step forward. He moved the phone away from his ear, convinced he could hear something. *Ringing?* The wind coming down the river whipped the sound away.

Then it stopped.

Going back to the phone, he heard Tyrone's voicemail message. He hung up and redialled, listening more intently.

This time he heard it. The ringing came from the bushes, somewhere behind him.

"Tyrone," he yelled. "Tyrone, are you there?"

Nothing. The ringing stopped as the voicemail kicked in again.

Marc cautiously retraced his steps and dialled again.

The sound came from behind a length of bushes that ran behind the footpath.

He stepped onto the grass that was sodden and waterlogged from last night's rain. Mud sucked and squelched at his feet. He hit redial once more.

This time the ringing was much closer.

The hairs down his neck and spine suddenly prickled.

Get out of here. Run.

Marc fought the instinct to flee.

Please God, not again.

The ringing came from under an overgrown section of bush. With a trembling hand, he eased a branch aside.

A slightly built young man lay in the dirt below it. He clutched a mobile phone in his stiffened hand. His eyes were open and unfocused. His skin was a ghastly shade of grey.

Marc recognised the same grim expression of death he had seen on the face of Dan Blumel.

The man's chest was a bloody mess of lacerations, so vicious and deep they had torn right through the padding of his coat and shredded the flesh beneath.

Chapter Nineteen

A Jagged Edge

Marc got up and stepped carefully away from the body. He was in shock but had enough awareness to know he was walking all over a crime scene. Too late to do anything about the contamination he'd already caused, but he could reduce any further impact. He rose onto his toes and attempted to retrace his steps backwards through the sodden grass. He didn't want to look at Tyrone's face again. It was an image that would haunt him for the rest of his life.

He looked around. On the opposite side of the park from the river, he saw someone. A man in a dark padded jacket, walking a dog on a leash.

"Help," he yelled. Then louder, "Help, please."

The man didn't even look in his direction. *Shit*. He was probably wearing ear-pods. Marc waved his arms above his head, desperate to attract the man's attention. He realised his urgency — he didn't want to be alone out here with a dead body — then he was immediately struck by guilt. What an awful thing to even think. A young man had lost his life. That's what he should be concerned about.

He dialled the emergency services. "Police," he hollered when the operator answered. "There's a body by the side of the river Bly." His voice was remarkably calm, given how badly his limbs trembled. He gave clear directions to where he was. The operator asked him to return to the body to check for signs of life.

"He's dead," Marc said. "I'm sure of it. His chest is all cut up. There is no life in his face."

Regardless, the call handler insisted that he check for a pulse.

Marc's feet became heavier with every step he took back. He closed his eyes as he drew aside the branch that covered Tyrone's body. His breath rasped through his teeth. He forced himself to look. Not at the man's slackened features, but at his hands.

Marc reached for his wrist.

Tyrone's skin was cool, but not completely cold. Whatever had happened to him, it hadn't been too long ago. Whoever had done this must have run through the park. If they had returned along the river, he would have seen them. Marc steadied himself and pressed his fingers to the radial point. All he could hear was his own blood in his ears. He concentrated harder, applied more pressure.

There was nothing. No pulse.

"I'm sorry," he gasped into the phone. "But's he's dead. There's nothing I can do to bring him back."

* * * *

Jason slid the box of tissues across the desk to his client.

Laura Moses was showing remarkable restraint, given the news she'd just received. She pulled a tissue, dabbed her eyes and gently patted her nose. "Thanks," she said, returning her hands to a careful position on top of her thighs. He never knew how cases like this would play out, but whenever he was hired by someone to find out whether their spouse was cheating on them, there was never a happy ending.

"How long has it been going on?" she asked.

"As far as I've been able to establish, about four years."

"Bastard," she said bitterly.

Laura had only begun to suspect her husband Ken's infidelity in the last twelve months. He'd obviously been a lot better at concealing his affair prior to that. Which meant one of two things. He'd got so comfortable in the deception, he'd become sloppy. Or he no longer cared about keeping it a secret.

She was a very attractive woman in her mid-fifties, with clear skin and thick auburn hair. Jason had seen her husband many times in the last four months, and even if he'd been much better looking when he was younger, he would still have been punching far above his weight when he married her.

Laura stared at him. "That's not everything, is it? I can see it on your face."

There was no way to sweeten this pill. He turned on his tablet, opened the photo app and slid it across to her. The woman in the picture was much younger than Laura or her husband. So far, so clichéd — balding and rotund middle-aged man with a much younger mistress. It was a textbook crisis for a certain kind of man over fifty. There were two children in the photo with the woman. A girl of around seven, and a boy.

"The girl is from a previous relationship," Jason said.

Laura looked closely at the photo. She gave an audible swallow. "How old is the boy?"

"Twenty-one months."

She let out a long, low exhalation. "That bastard." The sadness in her voice had been replaced with cold anger. "Any chance it could be another man's kid?"

"It's impossible to know without a paternity test, but…"

She glanced at the image again. "But the kid is the double of his fucking dad."

Jason didn't have to answer that. It was obvious.

"Does she know about me?" Laura asked.

Jason swiped to another photo. This one showed Ken and his girlfriend enjoying an alfresco lunch in the marina at Nyemouth, along the coast. "Her name is Michelle," he continued. "She's a probation officer." He zoomed in on the picture, closer and closer until Ken's right hand filled the screen. His fingers were bare. "He takes off his wedding ring when he sees her. She thinks he works offshore on the oil rigs, which is how he gets away with not seeing her for weeks at a time."

"And he tells me he's working away when he's with her."

Men like Ken were deplorable, but in a twisted way Jason had a degree of admiration for them. The planning, the deception, the sheer ability to remember the lies they told, had to take a staggering amount of effort.

He opened his desk and took out a large folder. "Prints of all the photographs are in here, together with my report on the times I followed him. I'll email digital copies too. It's up to you what you do with them."

She bared here teeth. "I want to stuff them down his fucking throat."

"Well, I can always get more prints if you do, but my advice would be to take them to a lawyer first. As far as I can establish, he has no idea that you're on to him. You might as well utilise that advantage and get in ahead of him."

She nodded, slowly. "That's exactly what I'm going to do."

Laura thanked him for all his work and gathered herself together. She left the office around quarter to six. Olivia had already gone, and he was surprised to find Ryman's office had been closed up too. He must have made plans with his daughters. It was the only reason he ever left early.

Jason stretched and winced at the pain in his chest. He was overdue a dose of painkillers. He got a glass of water from the dispenser and returned to his office to swallow two capsules. It had been a long but rewarding afternoon. Since accepting Marc's case, his other clients had taken a back seat. It had been a gratifying experience to catch up with some of them again, even though the updates he had provided hadn't been the best news for everyone. At least Laura knew what a deceitful piece of shit she was married to. Jason hoped she took him for all he was worth in the divorce.

He realised the time. Getting on for six o'clock. Marc had been due to meet Tyrone at four. His phone was in the top drawer of his desk. He always shut it away and put it on to silent when he was in a meeting.

There were seven missed calls.

Shit.

They were all from Marc.

Jason ignored the voicemails and called Marc's number straight away. When he answered there was a lot of background noise. People talking, sirens, traffic.

"What's going on?" he asked. "Are you all right?"

"Yes," Marc said. "Well, no, not really. But I'm fine. I'm not hurt. Did you get my messages?"

"No, I just finished with a client a few minutes ago. I called you straight back. What's the matter? Did you meet Tyrone?"

"Tyrone is dead. I found him by the river. He'd been stabbed. Just like Dan."

The world seemed to collapse beneath Jason's feet, like the floor had fallen away. He grabbed the edge of the desk. "Are you all right? Tell me, honestly. How are you?"

"I'm fine. I'm shaken, that's all. Fuck, Jason what is going on? Who the hell is doing this? Two of the boys we've spoken to in the last week are dead."

"Where are you? Are you safe?"

"Yes, there's a million police officers around. I've given a brief statement already, but they need to speak to me again in more detail."

"Where exactly are you?"

"I'm in the carpark at the concert hall. I found him on the path along the river. They can't get their vehicles down there so they're coordinating everything from here."

Thank God, he's safe. "I'm coming now. I'll be about fifteen minutes. Whatever you do, stay with the police. Don't go wandering on your own."

"There's no chance of that. Right now, they're treating me like a suspect. I've got an officer watching me like a hawk."

"That's good. Don't let them leave you, okay. I'll be with you soon."

Jason pulled on his overcoat. *Fuck.* This was escalating rapidly. His instincts were right. Two men had been murdered, and someone had tried to kill Marc and himself. Theo's death was far bigger than any hit-and-run. Someone was trying to shut the investigation down, permanently.

He grabbed his keys and hurried for the door, turning out the lights in his room. He should be able to get a cab from the rank along the street. With a bit of luck, he would be with Marc even sooner than he'd promised.

Ryman's office was in darkness and Olivia had shut down her computer on the reception desk. The kitchen lights were still on. He switched them off and checked the toilets to make sure no one was still in there. He was sure he was alone in the building, but it wasn't unknown for strangers to wander in off the street and use their bathroom. It was a matter of routine to check them before leaving each evening.

All clear.

As he hurried towards the top of the stairs, he froze, sensing he was not alone.

There was a figure on the staircase, halfway up. They were dressed entirely in black. There was a hood over their head and their face was concealed behind a black ski-mask.

"Who the hell are you?" he demanded.

The figure in black raised their right hand, revealing the jagged-edged blade of a hunting knife.

Jason considered his options in the fraction of a second. Another day, he could have taken them easily. He had the advantage of being above. A well-placed kick would send the stranger tumbling down the stairs. But with a sprained ankle and a broken rib, this was not an ordinary day. Could he really put up a fight, when a single punch to the ribs would incapacitate him?

The figure in black climbed the stairs.

Jason had no option but to retreat.

He stumbled backwards. Pain lanced through his leg as he put sudden weight on the injured ankle. He fought through it, making for the kitchen. His mind was already ahead of him, trying to work out what he would find in there that could be used as a weapon. There was nothing more dangerous in the cutlery drawer than a handful of forks and some butter knives. Useless compared to the hunting knife his pursuer wielded.

The same knife that had cut up Dan Blumel and Tyrone Lucas? Almost certainly.

Jason was determined that the blade would not be the end of him.

He heard the killer's footsteps at the top of the stairs.

Jason stumbled through the gloomy kitchen. The only source of light came from the landing. He yanked opened a cupboard.

The silhouette of the killer filled the doorway. Jason reached into the cupboard. All he found was a pile of plates. Better than nothing. He flung the first plate like a Frisbee, putting substantial force behind the throw. It missed the stranger by a foot, shattering against the wall. The debris clattered to the floor. Jason already had his hand on the second plate — he adjusted his aim and took another shot.

The killer was faster. They ducked and the plate sailed over their head and through the open door.

Before he could grab another plate, they were racing across the room towards him.

With a cry of rage, he swatted them as they came at him, landing a blow to their shoulder, but lacking the force required to do any damage. The killer drew back their arm and plunged the knife towards him.

A flare of lethal steel.

Jason jumped and rolled. He felt a rush of air as the blade just missed his arm. The pain in his chest was excruciating as he spun across the floor. Powering through, he staggered to his feet and rushed back the way he'd come. He snatched the handle and yanked the door shut behind him. It wouldn't lock but the delay to his hunter would buy him valuable seconds.

Rushing past Olivia's desk, he grabbed her chair and hurled it behind him. The castors rattled across the floor, crashing into the kitchen door just as his pursuer pulled it open. Jason kept moving. To glance around could be a disaster.

The adrenaline surging through him took the edge off his pain and he made it to the top of the stairs. He gripped the handrail and hurried down, two and three steps at a time.

Something heavy struck his back on the right side, sending a fresh surge of agony through him. He yelled in pain as the object banged down the stairs ahead of him. It was Olivia's laptop. There were footsteps behind him. Jason kept moving.

The killer had closed the front door when they came in.

Without a key, he knew it couldn't be locked. It could only be on the latch.

He reached the bottom and raced across the hall, already reaching for the lock, anticipating what he needed to do.

Then the instinct and intuition he'd learnt to rely on in the Navy kicked in. The killer was right behind him.

Jason spun and flattened his back against the wall.

His pursuer came too fast, and momentum carried them forward. They ran into the front door before spinning around, coming at him again with the knife raised.

At the last second, he ducked into a rugby position, ramming his good shoulder into their middle. Then he levered upwards, throwing them over his back, to land in a heap at the foot of the stairs.

The manoeuvre took him to the edge of complete agony. He had nothing left in him to keep up the fight. He had to get away before they got to their feet again. If they came at him with the knife, this time they would succeed in tearing him apart.

He grabbed the lock and twisted it off the latch. Racing outside, he pulled it shut behind him.

He scrambled in his pocket for the keys. He would lock the bastard in.

Too late. The latch clicked again and the door began to open.

Jason hurried out of the way.

The coffee shop next door was still open. There were a dozen or so customers inside, as well as staff.

As he staggered through the door, gasping in pain, struggling to catch a breath, most of the people stopped what they were doing and stared at him in astonishment.

"Police," he panted. "Call the police."

The killer was right outside. For a moment, their eyes locked through the window.

They can't be mad enough to follow me in.

A second seemed to drag for eternity.

Jason was not at all certain he was safe. This bastard was crazed enough for anything.

The spell broke. The figure in black stuffed the knife into their jacket and turned, fleeing in the direction of the bus station.

Jason collapsed in a heap as relief, pain and exhaustion overwhelmed him.

Chapter Twenty

An Unlikely Partnership

If Marc had given any thought to how it would be the first time Jason came to his house, he would never have imagined it would involve two police officers and take place in the aftermath of another murder attempt.

It was the morning after Marc discovered Tyrone Lucas' body on the bank of the river, and the near fatal attack on Jason at his office. When they had finally been released by the police last night, Marc had considered it safer to get out of the city and retreat to his house on the coast.

They were in the living room. Jason sat in the armchair with his injured leg raised on a foot stool. His eyes were deep-set and dark. His usually lustrous skin was wan and pasty. Marc knew he'd got very little sleep last night, despite the increased strength painkillers he'd been supplied with at the hospital. He was dressed in a pair of Marc's lounge pants and a loose T-shirt. They hadn't been back to Jason's apartment to collect any of his things.

Marc's parents were on the sofa. He was heartened by his mother's strength and determination. After what had happened to Theo, he'd half expected her to fall apart at the latest developments. She'd been more shocked that Marc had concealed the facts of Friday's car crash from her. She'd seen it on the local news and had no idea it had involved her son.

Marc sat in the chair across from Jason. His plastered arm rested in a sling.

He had met DS Benito Coppola before. The young detective was accompanied by the senior investigating officer, Detective Inspector Carina Glenister. She was a sharply dressed woman in her forties. Her dark hair was pulled into a tight ponytail.

They were perched on chairs carried in from the dining room.

Benito had made tea for them all before the DI got to business.

"I wanted to keep you up to date with what's happening in the investigation," the DI said.

Marc had already taken against her. She had an officious manner and insincere way of speaking. He'd met a million people like her in his business dealings. The corporate manager type who valved their own career ascension above everything else. There was no humanity to her tone. The caring attitude was forced and learnt more than felt.

"As of this morning, we are linking the murders of Dan Blumel and Tyrone Lucas, together with the attempts on your own lives, and with the unsolved death of Theo."

"Murder," Marc's mother corrected her. "It's not an unsolved death. It's an unsolved murder."

Marc caught the tightening around DI Glenister's eyes, before she sucked her lips and nodded sympathetically. This was not a woman who liked to be challenged. He wondered how many junior officers' lives had been made a misery on her route to the top.

"It's all part of one investigation," she continued. "DS Coppola has joined the major investigation team as part of our expansion. We've got a lot of officers working on the case now."

"As you should," Marc said. "Blyham police have let down the city once again."

Jason nodded. "Not to mention the LGBTQ community. Only weeks after the Blyham Strangler and you've got another killer targeting victims who have one thing in common — they're all gay men. Is that why you've drafted in Benito? Use your token gay cop to make a good impression."

Despite how tired and weary he felt, Marc couldn't help a small smile at Jason's opposition to the DI. He was entirely right. The city police force hadn't learnt a thing from the mistakes they had made during the Strangler murders.

"I can assure you that's not true," Benito said. "I'm joining the team because I want to find who is responsible for these attacks before they cause any more harm. The police force isn't perfect, but with scant resources, we do everything we can to protect the public."

"Excuses," Marc's mother muttered. "Do you expect all victims of crime to resort to the measures Marc has done? To hire a real detective to get to the truth."

DI Glenister looked at Marc and then Jason without moving her head. "About that. Yes. I'm going to need to see all of your notes relating to the case."

"I've already told you everything I've learnt. I found out more in a week and half than you lot discovered in three months."

"With respect, Mr Durham, it can be argued that your investigation has led to the death of two young men and the attempts on your own life."

Jason laughed at her. "Doesn't take much for your mask of concern to slip, does it? There we have it — the real face of Blyham police. Is victim blaming an active policy within the force these days?"

"I assure you that's not what I'm saying." DI Glenister tried to adopt a confident tone, but it was clear that she was rattled. "But policing is best left to the experts."

Now everyone in the room but the detectives laughed.

Glenister's cheeks flushed. She looked to Benito for help, who stared into his tea mug, ignoring her.

"Is that everything?" Marc said at last. "You told us you'd come to update us. Is that it? You've reopened the investigation into Theo's murder?"

"Well, yes. But that's not everything?"

"Do you have any suspects? Any CCTV footage from the river area yesterday? How far have you got with Dan Blumel's murder? Or finding out who stole the car that hit us." Jason's voice brimmed with anger.

"This is an ongoing investigation, I'm not at lib —"

Marc stood. "I think it's best that you go. We've been through enough, and you're not helping. In fact, you're making things worse."

Glenister was about to argue, but Benito was already on his feet and thanking them for the tea. Marc saw them out.

When he returned to the living room, Marc's father was gathering up the dirty mugs. His mother was at the window, watching the detectives leave.

"Are they all as bad as that?" she asked.

"What's the expression?" Jason said. "As useless as a marzipan dildo. That's how best to sum up Blyham police."

Marc sat on the arm of the chair and touched his face with his good hand. "Are you all right?"

"I'm fine. Apart from being tired, groggy, sore and, after talking to those two dipshits, pissed off." He took Marc's hand and brought it to his lips, kissing it gently. "But this makes it better."

"What happens now?" his mother asked.

"If we leave it up to that lot? Not much. They might shake down some of Tyrone's dodgy contacts and see if they can pin the murders on them. Or some random car thief might find he's being accused of a lot more than what he's actually done. But in terms of getting to the truth, it's up to us. We keep investigating."

"Oh, no you don't," his mother said. "Two attempts to kill you is more than enough. You might not be so lucky a third time."

"We have to," Jason said. "Whoever is responsible will keep coming until they're stopped. And I know we've got a much better chance of finding them before the plods do."

While Jason and his mother continued to argue, Marc sat back down and scrolled through his phone to the news pages. The murder at the river was getting a fair bit of coverage on the local news groups, but so far the police had withheld the name of the victim and the details of the killing. In the comments sections, people were making wild speculations about what was happening, including suggestions that the cops had lied about catching the Blyham Strangler, and that the real killer was still at large. They were also naming people with no connection, suggesting they were the victim.

Interesting, some people were also aware of the attack on Jason. Though nothing had officially been released to the press, there must have been enough witnesses in the coffee shop to get the rumours started.

Marc put down his phone and looked at the others. "Don't shoot this down until you've heard me out, but I've got an idea. You're going to hate it, but it might work to our advantage."

* * * *

"Why are you talking to me now?" Nadine Smythe sat at the kitchen table and extracted a mobile phone, notebook and pen from her oversized handbag. "What's changed?"

"You mean apart from almost getting killed for a second time?" Jason asked. He sat across from Nadine, looking a lot brighter than he had that morning. The painkillers seemed to have kicked in, but it was more than that. Since Marc had suggested his plan of action, Jason had perked up considerably. Having something to do had jerked him out of the depression that had threatened to descend on him.

"My parents know everything now," Marc told her. He put a cup of coffee in front of Jason and returned twice more with drinks for Nadine and himself before sitting down. "I tried to protect them from the facts of my brother's lifestyle. There was no need."

Nadine nodded. "I'm glad. I did always think you were overreacting. This isn't the 1970s. Parents are a lot more open-minded these days."

He let the little dig slide. They both knew she would have sensationalised every aspect of Theo's work, making it appear as sleazy and sordid as possible.

"But I still don't get this." She wagged her finger between the two of them. The red varnish on her long nails reminded Marc too much of the colour of blood. He'd seen more than enough of that in recent days. "You hate me. So why are you offering me an exclusive?"

"You've seen the latest headlines," Jason said. "The cops are giving nothing. They're going to sit on this until people forget it happened. They haven't even released details on the latest victim yet."

"I've already spoken to Tyrone's sister," Nadine said.

"You didn't waste time, then," Marc couldn't resist the snipe.

"I'm not going to write a hatchet piece, if that's what you think. The victims of the Blyham Strangler were barely a footnote in the reporting of that story. It was despicable. Tomorrow morning, my paper will feature a full tribute to Tyrone Lucas and Dan Blumel."

"It will?" Marc and Jason asked the question in unison.

"Yes," she said, defiantly. "Syrine Lucas, his sister, has given me her full blessing. Tyrone had a difficult life. Him and Syrine were dragged up as kids. Alcoholic mother, absent father. They were in and out of foster care for years, the only consistency they had was each other. He acted tough because he had to. People might look down their noses at online sexual content creators, but it was the first time in his life that Tyrone had a reliable job and income source. He had his struggles, and he deserved a lot better than a cold, premature end on a fucking riverbank."

There was a hereto unknown passion to Nadine's words, Marc would not have thought possible if he was not witnessing it himself. She actually cared about this injustice. A stark contrast to the cold-as-ice Detective Inspector that morning.

"And Theo?"

"Tell me his story and I'll write it up too. You can have full disclosure before it goes to print. Blyham police can't see the reality behind the victims. They're nothing but statistics to them. It's time to switch the focus and shame the bastards into action." Her eyes moved slowly between them. "Do you trust me?"

After a beat, Marc replied, "I do."

"So do I," Jason said.

"Good." Nadine fiddled with her phone. Her nails clattered against the screen. "I'll need to record this conversation."

They gave her a full and frank account of the last two weeks. How the search for answers to Theo's death had led them to Dan and Tyrone. They told her how they had discovered Dan's body at the gym after going there to talk to him. Jason gave his impressions of Tyrone. How likeable he had been beneath his tough talking exterior. She was especially interested in the botched attempt to run them down on Friday night.

"I don't fucking believe it," she said. "They didn't assign you with police protection after that. After what happened to your brother."

"Did you spot any officers out there on your way in this afternoon?" Marc asked. "After everything yesterday."

Her mouth tightened. "No. I didn't."

"Exactly."

"Shit." She scribbled in her notebook. "Do you have any kind of protection in the house?"

"I've got exterior cameras and an alarm. We're safe inside," Marc said. He wasn't worried about his security in the home. The killer had proved that they were far more likely to strike out in the open.

Nadine asked Jason about his experience the night before.

"Did you get any kind of impression about your attacker?"

"They were covered head to toe. Even their eyes were dark. And I was closing up the office at the time, most of the lights were out. They were fit, I know that. And fast. Hard to gauge their build given what they were wearing, but it wasn't some brick shithouse."

"Organised crime, do you think?"

"A professional hit, you mean. No, I wouldn't be here now if that was the case. If they were paid, they were strictly low-end. They've fucked it up twice."

"The type of person you might find hanging out in a grimy city gym?" she said. "Like the one where Dan worked?"

"It's certainly a consideration."

"What about Soloman Archer?"

"Another possibility, but we haven't got a shred of evidence against him," Jason said.

"And if he was going to hire a hitman, he could afford someone a lot more efficient and discrete than our killer appears to be," Marc said. The more developments there were, the less convinced he was becoming of Soloman's involvement. "He was seeing Theo as an escort, but he has no connection to any of the other victims."

"Unless they knew about him," Nadine said, "or had something on him. Something he didn't want to come out."

"But how long have you been digging into him?" Marc asked. "You haven't come up with anything and neither have we. He's a shit MP and seems to be a horrible man and vile husband, but I think he might be clear on this one. And Dan and Tyrone were killed with a knife, in a frenzied way. That doesn't suggest a professional assassin, does it? It's personal. I think this is someone killing for their own reasons."

"I still need to track down this photographer, Blake Remar. Tyrone thought he was dodgy, so did Theo's ex-boyfriend Roaul. Until we speak to him, he's still in the frame."

"So, what you're telling me is you've got nothing." Nadine closed her notebook and laid her pen on top of it. She picked up her coffee cup in both hands and sipped.

Marc and Jason looked at each other hopelessly across the table.

"It feels that way today," Jason said.

Nadine put down the cup. She reached across to take each of their hands. Unnerved by the nifty expression on her face, Marc accepted it cautiously.

"Then it's a good job we're all friends now, isn't it?" Her eyes rolled from Marc to Jason. "Because I'm an excellent investigative journalist and now is the time that you need my help."

Chapter Twenty-One

Alone in the House

When everyone had left and the house was quiet, Jason fell asleep on the sofa. It was dark outside when he woke up. Marc had switched on the lamps around the room and drawn the curtains. The local news played on TV. The volume was turned down low and the subtitles were running.

"Hey," Jason said. "What's up?"

"I didn't want to disturb you," Marc said. He was sitting on the sofa beside him, his broken arm resting on the edge.

"How long have I been out?"

"A couple of hours." Marc glanced at the clock. "No, more like three."

"Shit. I never sleep during the day."

"You needed it. That's why I didn't wake you."

Nadine had left around four. He must have fallen asleep straight after. "I wanted to make a start on the case. Call Blake Remar."

"Not today," Marc said kindly. "You can do that tomorrow. If you're up to it."

Jason was about to argue, then realised he barely had the energy to sit up straight. He was exhausted, in his body and mind. The painkillers must have made him drowsy, but they were wearing off. The hurt in his ribs and ankle was returning. He would resist taking another dose until bedtime. He didn't like the way they made him feel, and he couldn't afford to get hooked on them.

"Anything?" he asked, gesturing to the news report.

"Tyrone's death was mentioned as the fourth feature on the local news. Nothing on the national bulletin."

"Shit. This has overtaken our entire world and it's like nobody else even cares."

"Maybe now we've got Nadine on our side, it will improve."

"Do you trust her?" Jason groaned as he pushed himself into a more upright position.

"Absolutely not," Marc laughed. "But I think she was genuine today. She might be able to open doors that we haven't. And when it's all over, she'll definitely hold Blyham police to account, I have no doubt on that. She'll crucify them in print."

Jason nodded. "No one else is offering to help, so she's our best bet."

Marc switched off the TV. Though he'd spent the day fussing over Jason, Marc did not look in the best condition himself. His face was drawn, and his eyes were dull and dark. He looked like he needed a decent meal and a full eight hours' sleep.

Jason realised he was starving himself.

"How about something to eat?" he suggested.

"I'll order us a takeaway." Marc picked up his phone and tapped the screen.

"Not a good idea." When Marc gave him a puzzled look, he continued. "In case we find ourselves opening the door to our masked friend instead of the delivery. Unless your fridge and cupboards are completely bare, we should leave that as a last resort."

With a sigh, Marc tipped his head back to gaze at the ceiling. "Will this ever end?" he muttered.

"Yes." Jason patted his thigh. "It will. And we'll be able to do all of those normal things again. But until then, we need to take precautions."

They went into the kitchen and rifled through the options. Most of Marc's meat was frozen and Jason was too hungry to wait for anything to defrost. He found a dozen eggs in the fridge.

"How about I poach these? Quick, easy and delicious."

Marc protested, but Jason insisted he sit down and leave the cooking to him. He put a large pan of water on the hob to boil with a splash of vinegar.

"What you just said." Marc poured them a Diet Coke each and carried his glass to the table. "About things getting back to normal and being able to do regular things. Do you think that could include a traditional date sometime?"

"If that's you asking me out, then it certainly could." Jason cocked his head to one side. "Unless you plan on taking me to The Viaduct, of course."

Marc rapped his fingers in the tabletop. A gentle warmth had returned to his features. "Maybe we'll keep The Viaduct for a second or third date, eh? Let's not spoil ourselves all at once."

Jason kept the mood light and relaxed as he cooked, but deftly removed the largest butcher's knife from the knife block and placed it within easy reach. Somehow, he would attempt to take it up to bed with them later, hopefully without Marc noticing. When Marc excused himself to use the bathroom, Jason hurriedly double checked that the back door was locked. He'd confirmed the house was secure when Nadine had left that afternoon, but now darkness had fallen, he felt an extra sense of caution.

He put four eggs in the pan to poach and buttered four slices of toast. He'd always been an expert at cooking eggs and this time was no exception. When Marc cut into his and exclaimed delight when the yoke oozed all over the toast, he felt a small sense of pride.

"I've always been useless at poaching," Marc said. "I have mine fried or scrambled because I can never get them right."

"You'll just have to have me over to cook them for you again."

Marc's smile was the sweetest thing he'd seen all day. After so much angst and worry, its pureness went all the way to Jason's heart.

"You have an open invitation."

Jason cleared everything away and found a carton of chocolate ice cream in the freezer, which they had for dessert. Despite his injuries, the increasing pain in his ribs, and the worries of the last few days, this was as close to ordinary as anything he'd ever done with Marc. And he loved it.

He made tea and they sat talking for a while, before deciding they would go up to bed.

Excitement rippled through him at the prospect of spending a night with Marc, but it was tinged with restraint. They were alone in the house. And while its coastal location was idyllic, Marc's closest neighbours were a good distance away. They would have been safer back in the city. In a hotel, or Jason's apartment.

Marc seemed to read his mind. "All of the doors and windows downstairs are alarmed. There's no way for anyone to sneak in unnoticed."

Jason gave up on any pretence and picked up the butcher's knife. "I'll still sleep easier knowing we've got some protection up there."

They turned off the lights and headed upstairs. It had just gone nine o'clock and despite dozing for much of the afternoon, Jason wanted to go to bed. Marc went ahead of him. It was still a struggle to put weight on the injured ankle and Jason needed to take his time. He copped a look at Marc's fine arse as he mounted the stairs. It was good to know that stress and trauma had done nothing to dull his attraction for Marc.

In the bedroom, Marc turned on the lamps and shut the curtains.

"Any sign of a police watch?" Jason asked.

"Nah. It's desolate out there."

Jason opened the top drawer of the bedside cabinet and slipped the knife inside. "Just in case."

Marc came towards him, unfastening the buttons of his shirt with his good hand. "Can you help me with this?"

Jason grinned. "Try stopping me."

Marc untucked his shirt and Jason eased it off his shoulders, asking him to turn around slowly, to extract each of his arms. The bruises on his chest were a horrible, mottled fusion of black, blue and purple. Jason carefully put his hands on Marc's waist and kissed his collar bone.

"How do you feel?" he asked.

"It looks worse than it is." He shuddered as Jason drew his tongue along the hollow in his throat.

Jason unfastened the cord on Marc's sweatpants. "Let me help you with these too."

Marc stepped out of his slippers and let the pants fall to his ankles before kicking them to one side. Contained in a snug pair of white briefs, his hard cock inclined along his left hip. Jason smoothed his fingers across the bulge, feeling it twitch and lean into his touch. Marc sighed.

"I needed a hand with those as well," Marc said.

Jason slipped his thumbs into the waist and slid them down, releasing his powerful cock. As his briefs dropped, he cupped Marc's balls in the palm of his hand, gently juggling them in their sack. "Missed these," he whispered.

"And I've missed this." Marc fondled Jason's dick with his good hand. Jason groaned.

Jason dropped his own lounge pants and briefs with little effort. The T-shirt would not be so easy. Stretching through the ribs was too intense.

"I'm going to ride you," Marc said, brushing his cheek against Jason's.

"Can you manage that?"

"You're the one with the broken rib. I've just got this—" He waved the plastered arm. "Sit back and let me do all the work."

Jason climbed onto the bed and arranged himself with the pillows propped behind him. His eyes followed Marc as he opened a drawer and produced a bottle of lube and a box of condoms. "You might have to do this part yourself." Marc tossed him a condom. His cock bobbed as he got onto the bed.

Jason opened the wrapper and rolled the rubber down his dick, all the way to the root. Marc dribbled lube over Jason's cock, then coated its entire length, his good fist squelching with each pass. Another squirt of lube into his hand then his fingers went to his arse. Jason watched as Marc reached behind, pressing into himself.

"It's tight," he gasped, before throwing a leg across Jason's waist to straddle him.

"Are you sure about this?" Jason asked.

Marc didn't answer. He reached for Jason's cock and manoeuvred it into position behind him. The comfort of his crack pressed against the head before he found the opening. Jason put his hands on Marc's thighs, caressing him. Marc bit his lip in concentration, then lowered his hips, so slowly. He was tight. His hole was like a lock, refusing entry. Marc pushed down more insistently. It seemed impossible that Jason would ever fit in there, until there was a sudden give. His cockhead slipped past the resistance then the path was easy. Marc slid down his length until his buttocks rested on Jason's thighs.

They sighed with pleasure.

Jason couldn't take his eyes off his face. Marc's brow was furrowed, a blend of focus and delight. He licked his lips then drew a deep breath.

"I just need a moment," Marc whispered.

Jason twitched inside of him. "Take all the time you need. I could stay in your hole all night."

With a grin, Marc nodded agreement. "Not the worst idea I've ever heard."

Marc's cock was as straight and hard as a mast. His balls had drawn tight into their sac. Jason had no concern that Marc was in any discomfort. His cock proved just how much he was enjoying this.

When he was ready, Marc stayed true to his word. He worked Jason with his hips, rising and falling, just a little to start, before lengthening the motion, dragging his hole all the way to the head, before sliding down to the base. He did all the work, riding Jason for both their pleasure.

Pre-cum gathered on the head of Marc's dick. It glistened in the lamplight, before drooling down his shaft. He gasped and altered the angle of his hips, sending them both into fresh terrains of pleasure.

"Fuck, that's so good," Jason gasped.

"Mmm," Marc agreed. "It's filling me right up. I fucking love it."

This was a softer kind of sex than they'd experienced before. Jason wanted to grab him, flip him over and pound his arse into the mattress. Neither of them was in any fit state for that. For now, this was perfect.

Marc bucked and writhed on his dick — he bared his teeth and squeezed his nipples with his healthy hand. Jason couldn't take his eyes off him. The way his body tensed, how his cock bounced with the motion, scattering drops of pre-cum across Jason's belly.

"Now let me make you shoot," Marc said. He tightened his sphincter and adjusted the angle.

"Holy fuck," Jason roared as the movement took him to a new height of ecstasy. He reached a plateau. Marc held him there for what seemed an impossible age. Jason caught a breath and closed his eyes, then suddenly he tipped over and his cock throbbed inside Marc's arse, blowing one shattering expulsion after another.

He felt a hot gush across his belly as Marc squirted his own massive load.

Jason's legs trembled as the orgasm continued to course through him, shocking in its intensity.

"Fuck me," he sighed afterwards. "That was so intense. Amazing."

"No kidding." Marc panted, still rooted on his cock.

He wouldn't have believed it was possible, he'd been transported to another place. For a blessedly short time, he'd had no concerns about murder, or stalkers and who might be out there in the dark, wanting to do them harm.

Chapter Twenty-Two

An Unexpected Offer

Ryman had made a lot of changes to the office over the weekend. A security door had been installed at the foot of the stairs, denying access to the upper level for any non-approved visitors. An intercom and CCTV system had been set up on the reception desk. No one could get into the office without clearance.

"It's something we should have done a long time ago," Ryman said, showing Jason how the system worked. "There's also a camera on the front door and street, so we can check there's nobody lurking outside before we leave."

A week ago, Jason would have scoffed at these precautions. Not anymore. "I can't believe how quickly you've managed to do all this."

"A friend of mine from the rugby club runs the security company. He's been going on at me for years to take this up. When I told him what happened to you he agreed to work over the weekend to make sure we were set up for the start of business Monday."

"I'm very grateful. Really."

"Fuck that," Ryman said with good humour. "We almost lost you. Again," he added. "No more precautions. I'm putting a pause on all our other work, until this fucker is caught. Now come on, bring me up to speed."

They spent the morning in Jason's office, going over the case so far. He'd wondered how Ryman would handle the details of the gay sex work. He was a positive, open-minded guy, but some of the details of what Theo, Tyrone and Dan had been involved in, were out there. Jason had been shocked by some of it himself. Ryman was a complete professional, listening with compassion and empathy. His questions were all about the murders with no judgement on the victims. Jason felt guilty for thinking he would ever be phased by this.

The killings were the important factor. Not the details of the victims' sex lives or careers.

Olivia interrupted them around midday. "There's a woman outside. She doesn't have an appointment, but she says she knows you."

"Who is she?" Jason asked.

"Nadine Smith."

"Smythe," he corrected. "You'd better let her in."

Olivia pulled a sour face. "Do you really know her?"

"We're not friends, let's put it that way. But she's okay."

"She's a stuck-up bitch," Olivia muttered as she left the room.

Ryman cocked an eyebrow. "The journalist?"

He nodded. "She's agreed to help us. She said she would drop by and share what she has found out too."

Nadine strode in a minute later without knocking. She looked like she was made up for an appearance on morning TV, with a full face of make-up, big hair and shoulder pads. She shook off her umbrella and tossed it on the floor beside the door. "Does it rain all the time in this frigging city?"

"No. It only feels that way." Ryman introduced himself. They didn't shake hands.

Nadine plonked her oversized handbag on the desk and extracted a laptop. "Come on then, fellas. Show me yours and I'll show you mine."

Jason laughed. He would hate to be on the wrong side of Nadine's story, but he was beginning to warm to her.

"What do you know about Blake Remar?" Jason asked.

She perched on the edge of the desk. "Why?"

"He's a photographer who worked with all of the victims."

"Even you?" she asked with a vampy purse of the lips.

"I'm not a victim."

"*Yet*," she said. "The way things are going, that might be just a matter of time. Tell me about this guy."

"He was Theo's regular cameraman until they had some kind of falling out. It sounds like Blake got possessive and Theo didn't appreciate it. I've spoken to him on the phone, but he wouldn't talk. We need to get him to open up. He knows something he's not telling."

"And you think he's our guy?"

"Right now, he's just a person of interest. But it's a lot of interest."

Nadine's eyes sparked with delight. She reached back into the massive bag and pulled out her phone. "So, what's his number? I'm the queen of confessions. If he's got something to hide, I'll get it out of him."

* * * *

Marc went into the office for the day. Though he didn't want company or to have to explain what had happened to anyone, he didn't want to be alone either. He needed to be close to other people. On arrival, he told his assistant that he didn't want any calls.

"If anyone asks, I'm not here," he said, closing the door.

Jason had promised to call as soon as he had any news. Marc hadn't wanted to stay home by himself. It was crazy, but despite his high-tech security system, he no longer felt safe in his own house. He loathed that idea. It was the house he'd bought with Jack, the place they'd spent so many happy years together, and now he was spooked to be there on his own.

Marc twisted his wedding ring, thinking about Jack. As wonderful as it was to be developing feelings for Jason, Jack was always with him. The damn virus had taken him so suddenly. They had thought they had decades ahead of them, then he was gone. They'd never had a talk about what a future could be for one of them if the other was gone. Marc knew he was too young to realistically spend the rest of his life alone, but he'd had no interest in any kind of relationship until now.

He'd managed to satisfy his physical needs with a handful of random, emotionless hook ups, and had wanted nothing more than that. When one of those anonymous men had asked him his name, and a few of them had, he'd always lied. He hadn't wanted any kind of attachment beyond serviceable sex.

Now Jason had changed everything.

Of all the men Marc had fucked since Jack, Jason was the hottest. He was beautiful, tough, sexy. Those blue-green eyes could put him in a trance. But it was far more than sex. With Jason, Marc could relax. The circumstances could hardly have been worse, but yesterday, spending a quiet day at home with Jason had been very special. It had given Marc a glimpse of what his future could look like. Of a new beginning.

Jack would always be in his heart and with him in spirit.

But Jason could be with him in life.

The telephone rang, interrupting his reflection.

"No calls, please," he said. "Tell them I'm not here."

"I would, Mr Glass," his assistant, Cary said. "But it's Soloman Archer on the phone. You know, the MP. He won't take no for an answer."

Marc straightened up, suddenly alert. "Put him through."

"Mr Glass. Thank you for taking my call." The smooth voice of the politician was unmistakable. "I was shocked to hear what has happened to you. You're recovering well, I hope."

Marc's name had been kept out of the press regarding the recent incidents. Someone in Blyham police was obviously keeping the local MP informed. "Then you'll also know why this happened. In relation to the investigation into my brother's death."

"Another tragedy." Two words, steeped in insincerity.

"You knew Theo well." It was not a question.

"I was most distressed to learn of the accident. Your brother was a fine man."

Is this guy for fucking real? Soloman Archer was still in the frame for the murders and attempted murders. He might not have got his hands dirty himself, but it was a real possibility that he'd paid someone to deal with the inconvenience for him. Why was he calling now?

"I know all about your relationship," Marc said firmly. He wasn't going to dick around with this arsehole. If Soloman wanted to speak to him, it would be in full honesty. He didn't want to hear the political whitewashed version. "What do you want?"

"All right, I need to speak to you." The veneer of grace had vanished. He spoke in the cold, privileged tone of someone used to getting what he wanted.

"I'm only concerned with the truth. If you want to talk me into abandoning the investigation, you're wasting your time. It's gone beyond my own interest. The press is already involved."

There was a hiss of breath on the phone, and then, "Nadine Bloody Smythe. Look, it's in all of our interests to keep a lid on this. I want to help in your investigation and find out what happened to your brother, but it's best done in a mannered fashion. Look where barging around, asking difficult questions has got you. You've almost been killed once, and your partner has had two attempts on his life."

"You're well informed. If only the officers of Blyham police were as interested in solving crimes as they are in protecting you."

"I'm telling you, there's a better way to do this."

"Three men are dead. You can't make this go away."

"I know that, and I don't want to. I just want the whole matter resolved as quietly and efficiently as possible. Which won't happen if you allow Nadine Smythe to splash it all over her paper."

The police must have been watching the house yesterday after all. Nadine's visit seemed to have sent Soloman into some kind of panic.

"What are you suggesting?"

"Meet with me. I'm on my way to Blyham now. I should be there in a couple of hours. Come to my office around six-thirty. The staff will have left by then. I'll tell you all about my…acquaintance with your brother. Just hear what I have to say, and afterwards, I'll help you decide on the best course of action going forward."

He really is worried. Soloman wasn't due back in his constituency for another week. He'd obviously dropped whatever he was up to and rushed to Blyham. "You're only frightened of a scandal."

"Of course I fucking am. What the hell do you expect, man?" There was fury in the voice now. "When this all comes out, I want to be in control of the narrative. Helping you to catch your brother's killer is going to play a lot better than…well, the alternative truth. It's in my interest as much as yours to get to the bottom of this. Do you want to know what happened or don't you?"

Marc couldn't have detested the politician any more than he did at that exact moment. Soloman had something to hide, and the quickest way to discover what that was, was to go along with him.

"All right," he said. "I'll be there."

* * * *

As Nadine drove east, into the city suburbs, the bleak, late afternoon sky ahead was illuminated by a startling flash of lightning. Moments later, thunder boomed in the distance.

She gave an exasperated breath. "No fucking surprise. I feel like I'm living in *Blade Runner* in this bloody city."

"It's just the time of year," Jason told her. "It's a lot nicer in the summer."

"I've been here on and off for six years and you're talking shit. The summers are miserable too. If this story takes off, I intend to get out and I won't be coming back."

Jason smiled to himself. He was starting to realise that a lot of Nadine's toughness was a well-crafted act. He even suspected there was a nice person underneath it all.

She deserved her dues. Nadine had achieved what he'd been unable to. Blake Remar had agreed to talk to them. They were on the way to meet him before he changed his mind. Jason tried to stay positive, but with the way things had gone lately, he hoped Blake was still alive when he got there in order to talk.

"You've hit it off with Marc," Nadine said.

"And that matters because…?"

"Just an observation." She kept her eyes on the road. "I'm glad. Marc thinks I hate him, but I don't."

"You intrude on his grief and published photos of his husband's funeral. He's got good reason not to trust you."

"I'm a journalist. It was a newsworthy story. I had a duty to report it."

"I doubt he agrees."

"Even so, I'm glad to see him moving on."

The windscreen was peppered with a couple of heavy splats of water, before the rain came down in earnest. The wipers came on automatically and Nadine reduced her speed.

Jason kept quiet. What was happening between Marc and himself was nobody's business but their own. And he would not betray Marc's trust by spewing his emotions to Nadine Smythe.

His phone vibrated in his pocket. He pulled it out and saw Marc's ID on the screen. Nadine saw it too.

"Put him on speaker," she said.

Jason ignored her and answered. "Hi. Everything okay?"

"You won't believe who I've just got off the phone with," Marc said before telling him all about the call with Soloman Archer.

"There's no way he'd be here unless he was rattled," Jason said.

"That's exactly what I thought. I'm going to meet him as he asked."

"Whoa, hold on. Are you forgetting everything that's happened so far? Wait until I get back from seeing Blake."

"You've found him?"

Jason and Nadine had been in such a hurry to leave the office and get to Blake, he'd neglected to call Marc and fill him in. He gave him a brief update. "We're heading there now."

"You don't know what you're walking into either," Marc said. "Neither of these guys has been willing to talk to us, and suddenly today, they both change their minds. Do you buy it?"

"What's he saying?" Nadine demanded.

Jason relented and put the call on speakerphone. "Nadine can hear what you're saying," he said.

"About fucking time," she scolded. "So Soloman has slithered out of his hole. He must be shit scared."

"I agree," Jason said. "We'll turn around and come to get you. We'll speak to him together."

"No. You have to hear what Blake has to say too. We need to talk to both of them. You continue with what you're doing, and I'll see Soloman."

"He's got a point," Nadine said. "We don't know how long this is going to take and by the time we get there, Soloman could have changed his mind. I can't imagine his Parliamentary advisors know anything about this impromptu trip to Blyham. If they get wind of what he's doing, they're likely to shut him up."

"You see," Marc said. "This is the best way to do it."

Nadine swore at the driver in front of her, before yanking the wheel and pushing her foot to the floor. Jason winced in pain as he was hurled against the seatbelt. She completed her reckless overtake and swerved back into her lane.

"What was that?" Marc asked.

"Don't ask," Jason said. His mind was racing. What they were both saying made sense, but he didn't like any of it. "All right, stay where you are. I'll call Ryman and get him to pick you up. You'll need someone to drive anyway. It'll be safer if he goes with you."

"Good idea." Marc sounded relieved too. "Tell him to come for me now, I don't want to be late."

When he hung up he turned to Nadine. "What do you think?"

"Honestly? It's suspicious as fuck. Soloman is not an easy man to get to and he's just offered himself up. I don't buy it, but we can't waste the opportunity. Call Marc back once you've arranged his ride and tell him to record the whole thing, from getting out of the car. Don't ask the slimy bastard for permission, just get it on record."

Jason groaned. After two weeks of slow progress, things were proceeding at a rapid pace. Marc was in no fit state to put himself in further danger, but Jason knew there was no way he could stop him. Marc would meet with Soloman regardless of the risk.

The best thing he could do was offer some protection.

He took up his phone again and dialled Ryman's number.

He hoped they weren't all walking into an elaborate trap.

Chapter Twenty-Three

A Darkening Storm

The rain was pouring by the time they reached Blake Remar's address. It was as cold as stone on Jason's skin when he got out of the car. Nadine rushed ahead with an umbrella to the shelter of the porch, but Jason's ankle prevented him from hurrying. His hair was plastered to his head when he reached the entrance. He shook it off and wiped his brow with the back of his hand. Nadine had already summoned the lift and held the door for him.

The apartment was on the fourth floor. There was another boom of thunder as they waited for Blake to answer.

"Think he's legged it?" Nadine asked.

There was a click of a lock and the door partly opened. A face peered out from the guard of a security chain.

"Blake?" Jason asked.

"Let me see your ID," the man said.

Jason produced his wallet and complied. Nadine rummaged in her bag before pulling out her press card.

Blake squinted and studied them. He appeared uncertain. The door slammed shut. Jason was about to knock again when he heard the chain being undone and it swung open fully.

"Come in," Blake said without a hint of welcome.

His was in his early to mid-thirties. Blond and good-looking with a chunky build. He stood well back, regrading them suspiciously.

"The police have already been around," Blake grumbled.

"They have?" Jason wondered whether he had underestimated Blyham's finest, or whether they'd been given a hefty push from the local MP.

"They treated me like shit. Worse than shit."

"We're not the police, and I can assure you, we're not here to lay any blame. We just need to know what you know. You were close to several of the victims — "

"We weren't close. They paid me to do a job. They were clients."

"Even so, you know more about them than we do. Without even knowing it, you might hold the key to the entire mystery."

It was obvious from his face that Blake was not convinced.

"We're not looking to stitch you up," Jason said, with his hands out, palms up. "I took this case to help Marc Glass find out what happened to his brother Theo. Since then, two more men have been killed, and someone is also after Marc and me. We need your help, Blake. Honestly."

His gaze wavered between Jason and Nadine, until he sighed and nodded. "Come on through."

The apartment was large, with good-sized windows. The view might have been impressive, if it wasn't for the gloom of the storm. There were framed, poster-sized photographs on the walls. Most of them were black and white landscapes, though there were a handful of portraits. Jason recognised a picture of Theo straight away. It was a monochrome image that made him look like a matinee idol from the 1950s or '60s. Very handsome, with expressive eyes and a strong jawline. Far more classical than the usual sex images. For the first time, Jason could see the family resemblance between Marc and Theo.

"Excellent work," Jason said, making no effort to pretend he hadn't noticed the shot.

"He posed for that as a favour to me," Blake said, gazing at the image. "Theo wasn't interested in traditional photography or even glamour. All he wanted was content for his sites, but he agreed to this shoot eventually. I don't think he ever looked more beautiful. I wish he'd have allowed me to take more like his. He could have been a regular model, instead of just the sex work."

A gust of wind sent a burst of rain against the windows. Blake wandered across the room and stared out, avoiding their gaze.

"It doesn't sound like you were keen on the sexual side of things," Jason said.

"It's work. It came at a time when I needed the extra income. I couldn't afford to turn it down. I did it as a paid favour really. Put it this way, I never advertised shooting porn as a service on my website."

"Did you film a lot of men?" Nadine asked. While Blake's back was turned, she had turned her phone on to recording mode. Jason shot her a discouraging look. Nadine pulled a face and ignored him.

"Not if I could help it. I got on well with Theo, but most of those guys were more trouble than they were worth. They didn't always pay what they were supposed to, either." Blake turned around and dropped onto the sofa. "I don't do anything like that now. I don't have to."

"I've heard from a couple of people that you were fond of Theo," Jason said.

Blake stiffened. "Who said that?"

"It's not a criticism," he said calmly. "Just an observation. I thought if you were close, he might have confided in you."

"No. Theo did exactly what he wanted. He didn't come to me for advice."

"Did he ever mention having trouble with any of his collaborators?"

"No, he didn't, but I have eyes. I don't know what you think it's like to film one of these videos. It's my job to shoot the boys and edit it all in a way that makes them look sexy, like they're enjoying themselves and are into each other. That's not always the case. They come with egos and bad attitudes. Substance misuse. Mental health problems. Some of them make so many of these videos they're on the clock. Rushing to get it all done in forty minutes because they have another booking."

"So, are you saying there was friction between Theo and another model?" Jason asked.

"No," Blake snapped. "That's not what I'm saying. There's always tension, that's all. Just because they fuck, it doesn't mean they have to like each other."

"As fascinating as that is, it's not really telling us much," Nadine said. Jason winced. He didn't want her to piss him off and cause him to shut up completely. "Did any of these guys get violent or threatening?"

Blake's eyes hardened. *Fuck, she's blown it.* Then he softened again. "Not really. There was an argument between Tyrone and Theo over money, but it didn't amount to anything. And given what's happened, Tyrone is not going to be your killer, is he?"

"What can you tell us about Theo's escorting work?" Nadine asked. "Did he ever talk about that?"

"No."

"Did he tell you who he was meeting?"

"No. I wasn't interested. I took the pictures. I had nothing to do with his private work."

Jason realised he had no option but to pressure him. Time was tight and Blake wasn't telling them much that they didn't already know. "You didn't approve of some of the models Theo worked with."

"He could have done much better. He was degrading himself with some of those men. You only had to take one look at them to know they were trash. Theo could have done anything with his life. Look at how much his brother has achieved. Theo could have done that too, instead of taking it in the arse from guys who didn't deserve him." There was a crack of emotion in Blake's voice. "He didn't need to do any of that."

Jason couldn't work him out. He was kind of sad and exuded bitterness. From what he'd learnt of Theo, he would never have been interested in a man like this. Blake wouldn't have stood a chance. Could his jealously have driven him to kill the thing he loved, along with two other men? *No way.*

"These boys," Blake continued. "These content creators, they think they know everything. They think their dicks are so fucking huge they're the secret to their fortune. But none of them last. They burn themselves out. Everything they do has to be recorded and captured to keep up with the never-ending demand for fresh content. They can't even have a wank in peace because they need to film it. Theo put on a show of having a good time, he claimed he was owning it, but would have gone that way in the end, and I couldn't bear to watch that."

"I've talked with Roaul, Theo's ex. He said Theo enjoyed what he did. Tyrone confirmed it too."

"It was an act. When you work with these boys on a regular basis, you get to see the sadness in their soul. They develop a haunted appearance."

"I thought you said you didn't do a lot of this kind of work," Nadine said.

Blake gave a dismissive wave. "It doesn't take a lot. The erosion happens fast. Do you really think Theo was the first of the local models to die?"

Jason stiffened. Nadine crossed the room and stood over Blake. "What?"

"You heard me. Theo wasn't the first of the models to die because of this."

* * * *

Marc was glad Jason had insisted he wait for Ryman to pick up him before heading to Soloman's office. The older investigator had a clear-cut confidence about him that put Marc at ease. He was huge, from his head to his toes. Given Marc's broken arm, Ryman was a strong, physical presence. Marc had been pacing the floor, getting increasingly anxious about the call from Soloman when Ryman had dropped by for him.

He drove with the same kind of assurance, boldly overtaking and executing some serious manoeuvres in the worsening conditions. Ryman would get them to Soloman's office in the fastest time possible.

"You know he's done nothing for this city except serve himself," Ryman said, holding the wheel steady. "They're redeveloping that section down river to put in a new port. You know who the main beneficiaries of the contracts are? Soloman's brother-in-law and his best mate from uni. The man is as bent as a corkscrew."

"You're not a fan, then?"

Ryman's lips curled back from his teeth. "Can't say I'm a fan of any politicians, but when it came to Soloman Archer, the residents of Blyham couldn't have nominated a bigger piece of shit."

Marc did not disagree. At the height of the Blyham Strangler hysteria, Soloman hadn't made a single statement about what was happening in the city. It was peculiar that they had to rely on him now to shed some kind of light on the current spate of killings. If he could help them at all.

Marc had to remember that Soloman's sudden return and the offer to speak to Marc might be nothing more than damage limitation for the sake of his career.

Ryman found a place to park along the street from the office.

The rain was belting down when Marc got out of the car. It washed over the tops of the pavements. He shoved his plastered arm inside his coat and hurried towards the front door. It was closed when he reached it but unlocked.

Ryman followed him in.

The hall was gloomy. The lights had been switched off. The office must have already been closed for the day.

Marc headed up the stairs first. Though he already suspected this would be waste of time, he was keen to see his brother's some-time lover in the flesh. To figure out if there had been anything deeper between them than money and sexual transactions.

The reception desk was empty when they reached the top, and all of the lights were turned off.

Something was not right.

Ryman came around to stand in front of him. "Be prepared for anything," he muttered, looking around.

Light came through one of the doors that led off from the main room.

"Hello," Marc called out. "Anybody there?"

Silence, apart from the rain battering the roof and windows.

"I don't like this," Ryman said.

"No, neither do I." Marc's sense of unease reached the same level as it had when he'd found Tyrone by the river. Something was off. "Let's go back to the car. I'll call him from there."

A door to their right opened. For a few seconds, a figure was backlit in the frame before they reached out and flicked on a switch. The office blinked into light.

"Sorry, we didn't hear you arrive. You're a little early."

It was Soloman's PA, Chantelle. Her mood was so much warmer than the last time Marc had seen her. Typical. He'd met her type many times before in his own business. The kind who treated everyone with contempt until the boss was around when suddenly she was overflowing with charm. She wore a tailored black trouser suit with a silk blouse. Her hair was fixed in a smart upwards style.

"It's lovely to see you again." Her voice was full of charm, but her eyes were bereft as she shifted her focus from Marc to Ryman. "I don't believe we've met. Mr Archer isn't expecting a second guest."

"Ryman Blair."

Marc raised his broken arm. "Ryman is helping me to get around. And he knows all there is to know about our case. I'm sure it won't be an issue."

She was fighting the urge to come back with a rejection. Her smile stayed fixed and unmoving for what seemed like an age, then she said. "No issue at all. Trish has already left for the day. If you'd like to go through, Mr Archer is in his office. I'll bring some refreshments. Tea? Coffee? Something more grown up?"

"We're fine," Ryman said. His voice was curt, cutting through Chantelle's phony PR charm. "We appreciate how precious Mr Archer's time is. Can we get to it?"

She gave a closed-mouth smile. Marc could almost hear her silently counting to ten to retain her temper. "Go right on in. Mr Archer has been dying to meet you."

* * * *

Blake picked up an iPad. His fingers swiped and tapped at the screen. Jason and Nadine moved close enough to look over his shoulder. He pulled up a picture of a man in his early twenties. He had the same kind of fresh-faced, handsome features as Theo had had.

"His name was Stefan," Blake said. "I first met him on a legitimate modelling job, before he got into any of the sex stuff. He wanted me to take pictures for his portfolio."

Jason recognised the background in the next photo. It was taken from the river with Blyham Castle in the background. Stefan had his shirt open, revealing a toned and tattooed torso.

"But he didn't really have what it takes," Blake said.

"He's a nice-looking lad," Nadine commented.

"Nice looks aren't enough for a successful modelling career. He didn't have the star quality that agents and bookers look for. He was about twenty here. I spent an afternoon with him, shooting all kinds of images, and that was about it, until I met him again a couple of years after when he was doing the Hot-4-Fans thing."

The hairs on Jason's neck prickled. "Did he work with Theo or any of the other guys?"

"Theo? Definitely," Blake said, "I filmed one of their sessions. I don't know about Dan and Tyrone. Theo was the one who brought him in to see me. He was using a different name them, but I knew who he was straight away." He flicked to another image. "Stefan acted like we'd never met before, so I didn't make an issue of it. I figured he was embarrassed enough, and I didn't want to make things any worse."

"When did he die?" Nadine asked, impatiently.

"Last year sometime. Early, I would say. Like, spring. Maybe around Easter."

"And how did he die? Was it suspicious?"

Blake tapped the screen and pulled up Facebook. After a few more clicks he found Stefan's profile. "There you go," he said, showing them the tribute posts. "It was April. Suspicious, no. Stefan had major problems with substance abuse. When he came to see me with Theo he was a shadow of what he used to be. He died of an overdose. Deliberate, by all accounts."

Blake handed them the iPad so they could scroll through his account themselves. Jason clicked straight to the photo gallery.

"Was there a chance the overdose could have been murder and made to look that way?" Nadine asked.

"I'm not a detective. That's for you to find out," Blake said. "But I doubt it. The kid was in a dark place towards the end."

In most of the pictures, Stefan was a happy, good-looking boy. It was the usual assortment of social media images. Holiday snaps, birthdays, special occasions.

No different from anyone else his age. The most recent photo taken prior to his death showed a big family dinner. Jason guessed it was an Easter get-together. He was about to scroll to the next, when he halted. There was something about this group shot.

He clicked and enlarged the image, zooming in on the family members around Stefan.

"Shit!"

Right beside Stefan in that last photograph, smiling and raising a glass of wine, was a face he recognised.

"We need to stop Marc. *Right now*."

* * * *

When Marc and Ryman entered Soloman Archer's office, the MP sat in a high-backed chair, facing away from them. Only the top of his head was visible. Marc figured he was on a call. They approached the desk and waited, expecting Soloman to turn around and indicate whether he wanted them to sit or wait outside.

It seemed strange, after thirty seconds, that he did not speak or move.

That all too familiar sense of foreboding crept over Marc.

He looked at Ryman and realised he was having similar doubts.

Marc cleared his throat and said, "Soloman."

When there was no reply, he feared the worst.

He moved around the desk for a closer look.

The MP was held in position on the chair by cable ties around both wrists. His mouth hung open, his eyes were wide and unfocused. His shirt, from the neck down, was a wet, bloody mess. Marc gazed at the face of death for the third time since this investigation had begun.

"He's dead," he said.

As he raised his eyes to look at Ryman, he caught sudden movement in the room behind him. His mouth opened but had only half formed the warning when Chantelle swung a knife through the air and stuck it in Ryman's back.

Chapter Twenty-Four

Confronting a Killer

Nadine pressed down hard on the horn and cursed the driver ahead of her. The windscreen wipers were going full out as torrential rain battered the roof of the car. Though it was not yet dark, visibility barely reached three yards ahead of them.

Jason tried Marc's number again. It rang, and rang, before switching to voicemail.

"Shit," he swore through gritted teeth. The car came to a complete halt. "What now?"

"Red light," Nadine said.

At a standstill the force of the rain sounded like it was going to cave in the roof.

"He's not picking up," he groaned with frustration.

"Could be this storm," Nadine said.

He checked the screen on his phone. "Nah, I've got a signal. It's weak, but it's there."

"He's on the other side of the city. Maybe it's worse." She glanced in her rear-view mirror. "Shit."

"What?"

"Ambulance."

Jason looked behind. Through the rain-streaked window he saw the flashing lights. Nadine and the other cars in the line attempted to edge aside to make room for the vehicle to pass. It seemed to take an age to make its way along the road.

Jason took up the phone again and called emergency services. "I'm going to try the police. They'll probably get there sooner than we will." After Jason requested police from the initial call handler, the phone rang. It continued to ring the whole time they sat waiting for the traffic to clear. "They must be inundated because of the weather," he said.

The sound of sirens was right on top of them. The car was filled with the blue flash of the beacons.

Nadine took a deep breath and said, "Hang on."

As soon as the ambulance passed them, she jerked the wheel to the right and stepped on the accelerator, pulling into the road behind the emergency vehicle, following in the path it had cleared. Horns blared angrily around them. In other circumstances, Jason would have been furious at another driver behaving so recklessly. Not tonight. Whatever it took to reach Marc was fair and reasonable.

At the lights, the ambulance continued straight ahead, but Nadine turned left. Thankfully the road ahead was clearer.

The line to the police continued to ring.

"You're wasting your time," she said. "We'll get there before they even answer."

Jason swore again. He hated feeling this inadequate.

"Do something more practical," Nadine said. "Look up this Chantelle woman. See what you can find out."

He clicked through the search options. There was a profile page on Archer's website titled Meet the Team.

"Chantelle Readymarcher," he said, skimming the bland biographical details. "Friend of Soloman and his wife. Former campaign manager. Blah, blah, blah. Now his PA and responsible for running the Blyham field office."

He widened the search field and found an obituary for her husband. "Eddie Readymarcher, successful businessman. Married Chantelle in 2005 and adopted her son from a former marriage, Stefan."

"Did she kill the husband as well?"

"No," he said, continuing to read. "Cancer. There's no evidence that she's ever been involved in anything suspicious."

"Apart from working for the shithouse MP," Nadine muttered, tearing around a corner and narrowly missing an oncoming car as she veered into the opposite lane. She pulled to the left just in time to avoid a collision, slamming Jason against the door.

He gasped at the pain as the seatbelt locked against his injured ribs.

Nadine sped ahead on the clear road.

Jason glanced at the photographs of Chantelle Readymarcher. A woman in her mid-fifties, beautiful, immaculately groomed with lustrous honey-coloured hair and wide blue eyes. There was a clear resemblance to the images Blake had shown them of Stefan. The son who had taken his own life less than a year ago.

Was this respectable, conservative woman capable of murder?

The chill in Jason's spine gave him the answer.

* * * *

Ryman lay in a heap at Chantelle's feet. The efficiency with which she had killed him had been abhorrent. Six sharp and powerful strikes to his back. Ryman's face had contorted, then spasmed in agony, before slipping into an expressionless mask before he fell to the floor. Chantelle didn't flicker. The execution of a man—two men—hadn't caused a ripple of emotion.

In contrast, Marc's blood pounded through his body and sounded like thunder in his ears.

She gazed at him across the desk. Her eyes were stony. It appeared to Marc that she was dead behind them. The knife was in her right hand, held beside her thigh. Ryman's blood dripped from its lethal blade.

"I'd be correct to assume you didn't come here without telling someone else where you were? Your investigator chum." She sounded like a politician herself. Going on TV to announce a new policy or trade deal. Utterly emotionless and insincere.

Jason would surely come looking for him. Marc's phone had already rung twice in his pocket. It was set to vibrate so she wouldn't have heard it. He would need to take her by surprise in order to stand a chance. "Jason is on another case. I haven't spoken to him all day. Ryman has taken over the investigation."

"For a smart businessman, I'd have expected you to be a better liar. So, he's on his way now? Or can I expect him to turn up later?"

"I don't understand… Who are you? Why?"

In another political trait, she ignored the question. "I intended to kill you and Jason. If I'd been more on my game, you'd be in cold storage already. But Soloman, and this guy"—she jabbed Ryman with her toe—"they didn't have to die. You pulled them into this and now these two are all on you."

He trembled in disbelief. "Says the woman holding the murder weapon."

"Effective, isn't it. I should have just used this on you in the first place. It was over-ambitious of me to think I could get two for one with the hit-and-run. This" — she raised the blood-streaked knife — "has a far more successful hit rate."

Her voice hadn't modulated in tone or volume. It was like she was stating the most mundane fact.

"You killed my brother? You were the hit-and-run driver?"

She licked her lips and gave a short nod. "If I'd known then how much I enjoyed the knife work, I'd have finished him that way. But at the time, I needed it to look like an accident to avoid suspicion."

Marc was incredulous. She spoke without a scrap of remorse. There was no connection between the words and their meaning. Despite having just watched her murder Ryman, and standing before the corpse of Soloman, he struggled to make sense of what she said. "Why Theo? Surely not because of him." He gestured to Soloman.

"Him?" She seemed genuinely surprised by the question. "I couldn't give a shit about him. If the media found out what he got up to with those whores, that was his problem. I'm good at my job and would have lied convincingly on his behalf, but I wouldn't risk my own freedom for the sake of Soloman Archer. His wife might have killed him if it got out, though. Marianne knows exactly what he gets up, but as long as it doesn't reflect badly on her, she's fine with it."

Marc's muscles quivered with anger, and heat radiated all through his body. "Why did you kill my brother?" He slowly enunciated every word.

Chantelle cocked her head. "Why? Your brother was a vile, manipulative piece of shit. Your shitty sibling is the reason my son is dead."

He shook his head. "What the hell are you talking about?"

She showed the first flicker of emotion as her jaw clenched. When she spoke, her words were full of cold anger. "My beautiful son. *He* was a wonderful boy. He wanted for nothing and could have achieved anything with his life, until Theo corrupted him and dragged him into his sleazy affairs."

"I don't know what you're talking about."

"I don't suppose you do. Isn't that how you handled your brother? Sticking your head in the sand and pretending not to notice what he was up to. The porn. The prostitution. It embarrassed you, so you ignored it. Even now, this pathetic investigation you've been running was to protect your own reputation, was it not? Theo was filth. You know it as well as I do. Everything he touched was tainted. And eventually, that included my son. Your brother corrupted him."

She stepped around Ryman's body and paced the floor. The fingers of her free hand flexed repeatedly. She was losing that inhuman control.

As the room was illuminated by a flash of lightning outside. Chantelle didn't react. Marc doubted she'd even noticed it. She was lost in her head.

"Stefan died of an overdose. The damn coroner claimed it was suicide, but she knew nothing. Stefan would not have touched drugs if he hadn't met your slut of a brother. He needed them to numb the pain. For the shame of what he had done. Of what he'd become. A whore. Theo took someone wonderful and pure and dragged him into the gutter."

Who is this Stefan? The name had never once come up in all the time he'd been investigating. He couldn't remember Theo ever mentioning him. Neither had any of his friends or collaborators.

"I'm sorry for what happened to your son," he said. His voice was abnormally calm, given the situation. "I didn't know him, but whatever happened, does it really justify the murders of five other men? Shit, if any of what you're saying is true, Ryman and Soloman won't have even known him."

There was a sheen of sweat on her face. "Ryman, okay, yes. Soloman, I'm not so sure. I haven't found any evidence, but with all the other shit he's into, I wouldn't put it past him. He might not have known Stefan was my son. I doubt it would have bothered him anyway."

"You're mad. Can't you hear how insane this sounds?"

"Mad? Is it mad for a mother to love her son? To want to protect him from corrupt abusers, Soloman and your brother?"

"You seemed happy enough to have turned a blind eye to what Soloman's been up to all these years. Is it only abuse when it involves someone that you love?"

"I don't take any pleasure from what I have to do." She had regained her confidence. She stood straight and defiant. Her features composed. Even her eyes had lost their madness, replaced by steely determination. "I only ever wanted justice for my boy. Your brother and those disgusting friends of his, they would have been enough. If you hadn't gone snooping in things that don't concern you, no one else would have had to die."

Her knuckles tightened around the handle of the knife, and her tight-lipped smile sent a chill through Marc that went all the way to his soul.

* * * *

"Pull up at the end of the street," Jason said. "I don't want to tip her off that we're here."

"I'm coming in with you," Nadine argued.

"No," he said firmly. "I need you to keep trying the police. And watch the office. If she comes out without us, follow her."

Nadine seemed on the verge of disagreeing, then closed her mouth and nodded. She turned the car into the terrace and pulled up to the kerb, four properties down from Soloman's office. The rain made it just about impossible to see, but through the rapidly wiping blades, he made out a light in one of the upstairs windows.

"What are you going to do?" Nadine asked. "She got the better of you once before, remember."

"She took me by surprise. This time I have the advantage." He put his hand on the door. "Keep calling the cops, okay. We're going to need them."

Nadine already had her phone in hand.

Jason stepped out. A surge of water washed clear over the gutters. This was the worst storm he could remember in years. The river Bly would burst its banks if it kept up for much longer. He pulled his jacket up to his throat.

Ryman's car was parked farther along the street. They were still here, then. Talking to Soloman? Or had it been a trap orchestrated by his PA?

Jason reached the front door. He tried the handle, relived to find it unlocked. He couldn't remember whether there was a bell to alert the office upstairs whenever someone entered. *Damn it.* He'd have to take the risk. Opening the door, he rushed inside and closed it behind him. To his relief, it didn't appear rigged to an alarm.

He pressed his back against the wall and waited, listening. Even without a ringer, it was possible anyone upstairs would have heard the increasing noise from the storm as he made his way in. He counted slowly to ten.

Nothing.

Jason advanced. On just the balls of his feet, he went up the stairs.

As he approached the top, he flattened himself against the far wall, to give him the widest view as he came up. The reception area was empty.

He heard voices and immediately recognised Marc.

The light he'd seen from the street came from an office at the front of the building.

He proceeded carefully. The top step creaked as put his weight on it.

Jason froze. Waited.

After another few seconds, when there was no movement from the office, he crept into the reception room.

There was no one at the desk. He checked behind it, in case somebody should be lurking there. It was clear. Whoever was in the building, was in that front room.

Was he overreacting? He hoped so.

It would be a relief to open that door wider and find Marc and Ryman chatting around the desk with Soloman.

Instinct, combined with years of experience, told him otherwise.

Breathing shallowly, Jason moved across the floor. He strained to hear.

"Did your son ever talk to you about any of this?" It was Marc's voice. There was something off about it. A note of false bravado.

"Of course he didn't." Chantelle. So, their suspicions were correct. "He would still be here otherwise. His problems wouldn't have seemed so bad if he'd confided in his mother."

The door was open by just over a foot. He could barely make out the room beyond.

Jason edged closer.

Marc was on the far side of the desk. His hands were raised before him in surrender.

Where the fuck is Chantelle?

"Those other boys all had mothers too," Marc said. "Theo, Dan and Tyrone."

"No. They were sons of fucking bitches. Stefan was better than any of them. And their mothers deserve every agonising second of grief they suffer, and it will never come close to my own pain."

From the sound of things, she was a metre or so in front of the door, still out of sight.

Where was Ryman? Jason couldn't see or hear anything of him.

He weighed up the options.

Rush in, in the hope he could tackle her. Surprise was on his side. His injuries might prevent him from fully overpowering her, but with Marc and Ryman's help, she wouldn't be a problem. But what about Soloman? Was he in there too? Was he on her side?

Fuck.

If he knew the cops were on the way, he could just walk in and say so. They should be able to contain her until they arrived.

But in this weather, with the roads as bad as they were and services stretched all over the city, he couldn't count on it.

Surprise was the greatest weapon that he had.

From his current position, it was his only option.

He fixed himself, took a deep breath for fuel, then charged at the door, flinging it wide.

Chantelle stood across the desk opposite Marc. As she turned in surprise, Jason was already pounding towards her. He had speed and trajectory just right. He would take her down.

She raised the knife.

He was still on track to stop her.

His foot touched the floor and as he powered forward, he slipped. The wooden floor was wet. Jason's feet went out from under him, and he lost momentum. Chantelle ducked aside and he hit the front of the desk with full force. He roared in agony as pain from his injured ribs tore all through his body.

Jason dropped to the floor.

The world became a kaleidoscope of crazy images. As he hit the ground, he looked straight into the slackened face of his partner. There was blood all around them. Survival instinct impelled him to move. He rolled onto his back.

Chantelle was right above him. Her lips moved but he couldn't understand a word.

Her knife drew back, and she was coming at him.

Jason couldn't get away. This time the pain was too great.

He prayed Marc would use the distraction to escape. If this was the end, it would be a consolation to know he got away.

Chantelle came closer and the knife bore down towards him.

Then another movement. Marc was right behind her. He swung hard, smacking her across the head with his plastered arm. She was lifted clear off her feet.

Jason's vision dimmed. He fought against the blackout.

Marc was above him. Tapping his face, shaking his shoulders.

"...up."

Jason winced. His sight and hearing were woozy, but were returning.

"Where is she?" He tried to sit up, which triggered another rush of darkness. He paused a moment before continuing. The pain in his chest was agony. *Probably broken another rib.* "The knife."

"I've got it," Marc said, helping him to lean against the desk. "She's gone. But I think she's locked us in."

"Are you all right?"

"I'm fine," Marc said.

Despite their situation, Jason felt a sudden lightness of relief. He gripped Marc's good hand, wanting to hold him. Needing a moment of stillness to let it sink in. He raised Marc's hand to his lips and kissed it. When this was over, he wanted to hold him and never let him go.

"Can you stand?" Marc asked. "If she's locked the door, we're not out of trouble yet."

Jason nodded grimly. He gritted his teeth and when Marc counted to three, together they managed to get him to his feet. Jason sucked in a great mouthful of air.

It was then that he smelled burning.

Looking towards the doors, he saw grey tendrils of smoke creep under the bottom.

Chapter Twenty-Five

Ablaze

"She's set fire to the place," Jason said.

"Stay here," Marc told him, easing him against the desk. Jason was in a bad way. The howl of pain he'd issued when he'd gone down made it clear that he'd sustained further injuries.

Marc hurried to the office door and tried the handle. *Shit.* It was locked. He gripped with his good arm and rattled the knob. Hopeless. It wouldn't budge.

Coils of smoke crept through the cracks between the door and the frame. What was she trying to achieve? Destroying evidence. She couldn't be deluded enough to think she would get away with this now. Four people dead inside a locked room would arouse plenty of suspicion, regardless of how she tried to disguise it. If she was thinking rationally at all. What he'd glimpsed in her eyes while she stabbed Ryman was completely deranged.

"What happened?" Jason asked. His body slumped as he took in the corpse of his friend and partner.

"Soloman was already dead when we got here. She took Ryman by surprise when we found his body."

Marc crossed to the window. He threw it open, but it was attached to a safety device that only allowed it to slide six inches. He could smash it easily enough with one of the office chairs. In normal circumstances, they would both be fit enough to hang down and drop to the ground below. But with their current injuries, they had no chance of making it.

He glanced at Jason. He was in a bad way, but a few more broken bones would be preferable to being dead.

"Did you notice a fire escape?" Marc asked.

Jason shook his head, wincing as he pulled his phone out of his pocket. "I doubt it has one. It's just a row of terraced houses converted into office space." He put his phone onto speaker and dialled, getting an immediate engaged tone. "Shit. Emergency services are all tied up with the storm. I tried to reach them on the way here."

There was another door on the far side of the room. Marc went through into a bathroom. There was a skylight above the toilet. It offered a glimmer of hope. He climbed onto the seat and pushed the window open. Wind and rain whipped straight through, clawing at his face. Marc pushed his head and shoulders outside, assessing their options. If they could make it to a similar skylight in one of the neighbouring buildings, there could be a way down. The roof was slanted, and the tiles were perilously wet. There was every chance that they would break even more bones if they tried to get out that way.

When he returned to the main room, the smoke was thicker than before. He coughed as it seared his throat and eyes. Chantelle must have used some kind of accelerant to get the fire going so quickly. She must have planned this. When had she decided to kill her boss? Today? When he said he was returning to Blyham early? If this was premeditated, then she must have also planned her escape.

No fucking way. She was not going to get away with hurting so many people.

"We have to get out of here so we can nail that bitch," he said.

"I won't argue with that." Jason hobbled to the window and looked down. A gust of rain battered the pane. "It doesn't look like we've got another option. We'll have to go this way."

Marc put his arm across his face as the smoke grew more acrid. "Can you even make it that far? You're in a bad way already."

"A few broken bones are better than being burned alive."

Jason's practical manner and cool headedness was an almighty reassurance. Marc realised at that moment that he would trust him whatever happened. There was no one better to have on his side during a crisis.

Smoke continued to billow into the room.

"That door isn't going to hold it back for much longer," Marc said.

"Then let's get out of here. Take off your jacket." Jason was already shrugging his waterproof off his shoulders. He grimaced at the discomfort.

Marc didn't understand but did it anyway, slipping out of his coat.

"Get Soloman's and Ryman's too."

"What are you going to do?"

"Think of it like a prison break. We'll knot them together to make a rope. It won't be enough to get us

all the way to the ground, but it will lessen the drop."
He took Marc's jacket off him and made a hurried knot
with their sleeves.

Turning to Soloman, Marc was filled with revulsion.
Chantelle had made a mess of his chest and throat.
How could she have been filled with so much hatred
and anger? The doggedness to have done this to
another human was unfathomable. He found a pair of
scissors in a drawer and cut the cable ties on his wrists.
"I'm sorry," Marc said, easing Soloman's corpse
forward in the chair to shrug the jacket from his
shoulders. He was heavy and difficult to manoeuvre.
As the smoke poured into the room, there was no time
to be squeamish. He got the jacket free from one arm,
then the other and passed it to Jason.

However difficult it was to deal with Soloman, it
was nothing compared to what he had to do next.
Ryman lay on the floor, on his front. The back of his
jacket was soaked with blood. Despite the repeated
injuries, the structure of the garment seemed sound.
Marc carefully eased it from his body. "I'm so sorry,"
he said, fighting a coughing fit. "We won't let her get
away with this."

The last thing he did was place his index finger and
thumb over Ryman's eyes and pull them closed.

He gave the last jacket to Jason for him to tie with
the others.

The smoke was becoming overwhelming. They
crouched low to the ground as it filled the room.

Jason tied the sleeve of his impromptu rope to the
top of a radiator.

There was a paperweight on Soloman's desk. Marc
took it in his good hand and assessed its heft. It should
do. They were running out of other options.

"Stand back," he warned Jason.

He angled from the waist, getting as much power behind the throw as he could and hurled the weight at the window. It broke through, shattering the glass from the top of the frame to the bottom. Marc picked up a table lamp and used it to smash away the jagged shards, until the window was clear. He gasped for fresh air.

"Over you go," Jason said.

"No. You're in worse shape than I am. You go first, I'll be right behind you."

"There's no time to argue," Jason shouted. "I'm more used to climbing than you are. Get out."

There was a loud, splintering crack in the room behind them. The door was giving way. Marc could barely see an arm's length behind him for the smoke.

"Use your good arm and legs," Jason said with a cough. "Keep going and don't stop."

Marc swung his leg over the window. "You'd better be right behind me, or I'm coming back for you."

"You can't keep me away from you. Move."

The pain in Marc's arm became a minor concern. He gripped the jacket rope with his uninjured arm and thighs, wrapping his broken arm around it and shimmying down with a speed he wouldn't have thought himself capable of. The rain turned the outer coating on his plaster to a slimy mush, but Marc had more critical concerns. At the bottom of the rope, he dangled down as far as he could stretch before dropping to the ground.

He was instantly on his feet, shaking rainwater from his eyes to track Jason's progress.

Despite his extensive injuries, Jason climbed out of the window and flew down the rope even faster than he had. He landed at the bottom with an uncomfortable grunt.

"Are you okay?" Marc gasped. "Are you all right?"

Jason pressed his mouth against Marc, crushing his lips in a breathless kiss.

They were alive and it was the only answer he needed.

* * * *

Marc had spent far more time in the emergency rooms of Blyham hospital in recent days than he cared for. In the last three hours he'd been treated for smoke inhalation and had the plaster cast on his arm reset. He'd been discharged and waited in a side room with Jason. Jason had been to the X-ray department and had confirmation of another broken rib.

It was only now, sometime later, that the full impact of what they had been through settled upon them. Marc held Jason's hand. The hospital was a riot of noise and action, but behind the curtain they were alone. Neither of them had spoken in a while.

There was no need. They'd lived through the experience and knew exactly what had happened. The hospital was also crawling with police. There was a uniformed guard standing right outside the cubicle. Protection, in case Chantelle attempted to finish the ghastly job she had started.

They both looked up as the curtain was torn aside. It was Nadine. Her usually immaculate hair was waterlogged. Her suit was sodden and crumpled.

"Any news on Ryman?" Jason asked. His voice deeper than usual.

"They've put out the fire," she said. "But as far as I know they haven't extracted their bodies yet. The police have already notified their families."

"Oh, hell," Jason groaned. "Poor Karina. She'll be devastated. They have two kids, too."

Marc's heart ached with sadness. He squeezed Jason's hand a little tighter. If he hadn't instigated this investigation, his friend would still be alive. So would three other men. He knew that none of this was his fault. Chantelle was responsible for all that had happened, but it didn't lessen his guilt.

"Any news about her?" he asked. "Has she been sighted?"

Nadine shook her head. She had seen the killer flee from Soloman's office, but by then Nadine had realised that Jason and Marc were in trouble. The flames were already obvious at the windows and Nadine couldn't have followed her.

"Everything Blake told us checks out." Nadine handed Jason her phone.

Marc leaned in to see the screen. Nadine had pulled up a news story accompanied by a photo of a fresh-faced young man.

"His suicide barely got a mention, just a tiny feature on the local news group. Stefan Readymarcher killed himself last April, after a long period of depression. It's a tragic story but not enough to go beyond local interest. Chantelle doesn't even get a name check."

"Survived by his mother," Jason read aloud.

"He was her only child. From what I've been able to find out, he dropped out of uni when he was twenty, to pursue a modelling career."

"He was a good-looking boy," Marc remarked. Stefan Readymarcher reminded him a lot of Theo when he was younger.

"He took after his mother," Nadine said. She perched on the edge of Jason's trolly. "She tried to be a model when she was younger, too. I'm guessing she encouraged him. Obviously not with the Hot-4-Fans stuff, but she must have fancied his chances in the mainstream industry."

"How do you know this?" Marc asked.

"It's easy enough when you know where to look. That was the problem before. No one was even looking at her. We thought, if anything, the killer was going to be some kind of dodgy connection on Soloman's part. Not his glamourous PA."

"How did she managed to kill four men? Four strong, well-built guys," Jason asked. He looked and sounded exhausted.

"I saw what she did to Ryman," Marc told him. "Trust me, she's capable all right."

"I have no doubt about it," Nadine said. "We've got a team going through every damn thing she's ever posted online. In the morning they'll start knocking on doors. From what we know so far, she used to work at the box office of the Empire Theatre while trying to get her modelling career off the ground. When it didn't, she married a playboy businessman called Des Carlisle."

"Des Carlise?" Marc said incredulously. "I know him. He went bankrupt years ago. He even owned me money at one time."

"Chantelle ditched him before things got that bad and upgraded to Eddie Readymarcher, who was older and even richer. He also adopted the kid she had with the first husband, Stefan. Readymarcher died about five years ago, leaving her very wealthy. Which is when she helped Soloman Archer with the campaign that led to him winning the local seat. She had no need to work, but it appears she liked the status that went with working for a member of Parliament."

"Until she stuck a knife in him," Jason grumbled.

"What about Stefan's Hot-4-Fans account?" Marc asked.

"Everything checks out. Chantelle had the account deleted after his death, but nothing ever really disappears from the internet. He promoted his videos on Twitter and the clips are still there. Including one with Theo."

"Shit. Can we get them removed?"

"I had already put in requests on your behalf," Jason said. "Theo's stuff should be gone very soon."

"She killed four men because of a few raunchy clips?" Marc said incredulously. "It doesn't make sense."

"I think it was more to do with the corruption of her precious child," Nadine said. "It looks like Stefan had issues before he ever got involved with Theo. But when has rational thought ever stopped a parent from doing whatever it takes to protect their kid?"

"It's such a waste," Jason said. Marc had never heard him sound so sad or dejected. His pallor was even more washed out than before.

"Are you feeling okay?" Marc asked. "Want me to get a doctor?"

Jason looked straight at him with wide, wounded eyes. "I'm just sick of this shit. Four men have died for nothing. *My best friend has died for nothing.*" Tears spilled over the lids and streaked through the smoky deposits that coloured his cheeks. "I almost lost you."

Marc got to his feet and leaned over the bed. He hugged him gently. He really wanted to wrap his arms around Jason and hold him until there was no more hurt, but pain was a grim reality. Physically and emotionally. Marc pressed the side of his head against Jason's. He kissed him on the neck. "You haven't lost me. She could never take me away from you."

Then his own tears came, and he made no attempt to stop them.

Chapter Twenty-Six

A City in Mourning

Three nights later, the streets of Blyham were brought to a standstill by a procession that started on the riverside, in front of the Vermont Hotel, where Theo Glass had been killed by Chantelle Readymarcher four months earlier. Thousands of people gathered, carrying photos and candles, to honour the victims. The parade passed along the waterfront before heading upwards through the centre of the city to gather before the town hall at eight p.m.

It was a predominantly solemn and heartfelt occasion, but there was anger too. Among the tributes to the deceased, there were placards reading *How Many More Must Die? Shame on Blyham Police* and *Stop the Killing Now.* There were Pride flags and LGBTQ+ banners but the sadness and anger that were felt in the city went far beyond that community. There was fear across all social groups as people wondered which minority would be targeted next.

Marc and Jason waited at the town hall for the parade to arrive. Neither of them was fit enough after what they'd been through to complete the route on foot. Marc's parents sat beside them. They were both in tears, holding hands as they witnessed the shared grief of so many people. Theo's face was displayed prominently on placards and T-shirts as the people of Blyham honoured the dead.

The police were there to monitor the crowds but kept a respectful distance. Marc knew how strong the anger in the city was towards them. One wrong move and this peaceful protest could tip into a riot. The media interest in the march was off the scale, with TV news crews and reporters battling for position in a sectioned off area in the square. They'd been warned not to provoke the mourners. Anger towards the press was almost as strong as that towards the police. None of the victims had been deemed newsworthy, until the killing of Soloman Archer had made the story a national sensation.

Only Nadine Smythe had been granted a place beside the families and friends at the front.

The tension was a dense, palpable thing, but as he looked upon the sea of people, at the candles and messages of love, Marc felt a sad sense of optimism.

"It's beautiful," he said, almost choking on his pain.

Jason put a gentle hand on his thigh and squeezed encouragingly. "It can sometimes take the worst to bring out the best of people."

The mood this evening could have been a lot more hostile, where it not for the fact that Chantelle had been apprehended. She'd been caught at the Port of Tyne the day after the fire at Soloman Archer's office, attempting to board a ferry to the Netherlands on a passport she had stolen from her housekeeper. The housekeeper had fared better than her other victims, having been discovered by the police beaten, tied up and gagged at her home. But, unlike the others, she was alive.

Chantelle had been charged with five counts of murder, two attempted murders and arson with intent to endanger life. After a brief appearance at the magistrates' court, she'd been remanded in custody and would appear at Blyham Crown Court in a few weeks' time. There would inevitably be a trial. Marc harboured no hope that she would plead guilty. A trial would mean recounting everything that had happened all over again. What did he care about that? He would tell his story a million times over if it meant that evil woman spent the rest of her life in prison.

The crowd in the square continued to swell and showed no sign of stopping. There must have been several thousand people there already. As the sky darkened into dusk, the candles and tealights took on a more poignant, ethereal aspect.

As touching as the display was, Marc would give anything to have his brother back instead. For each of the victims to be alive and enjoying the love of their families and friends.

The emotions he'd managed to keep a tight lid on all evening suddenly broke. As a sea of lights flickered in front of him, the tears poured down his face.

Jason put an arm around his shoulder and leaned into him.

He didn't need to say anything, his touch was enough.

* * * *

Three hours later, Marc stood on the balcony of Jason's apartment, staring at the cityscape. His eyes were cried out and his throat was raw from all the sobbing he had done. The vigil had unleashed so much pent-up grief. As he'd broken down before the crowd of strangers, he'd realised it was the first time that he'd truly missed his brother. He hadn't even cried at Theo's funeral. He'd had to keep it together for the sake of his family and to ensure that all their wishes had been fulfilled that day.

And afterwards, he'd carried on as normal. Back to work. Back to his routine.

If it hadn't been for Nadine threatening to expose Theo's lifestyle, would he have continued to get by, content in the knowledge that his brother had been killed by a hit-and-run driver who would likely never be caught?

It pained him to accept that the answer was yes.

"I'm sorry," he said, looking to the night sky. "Little brother. I should have done so much better for you."

The door behind slid open. Jason came onto the balcony carrying two crystal tumblers of whisky. He raised a tired smile in the evening light. The last few days had been hard on him too. Marc was not the only one choked with grief. Ryman had been more than just a business partner to him, more than just a friend. They had been like brothers themselves.

Despite his exhaustion, Jason looked incredibly handsome. Like Marc, his eyes had been cried dry.

Marc gratefully accepted the glass.

"Are you okay?" Jason asked.

He nodded. "I don't think it will get easier just because we know the truth, not for a long time, but uncovering the truth is a start. Right?"

Jason came close. He leaned in and kissed him on the mouth. "We'll get through it. We'll do it together."

Marc smiled. They stood side by side, gazing at the city. He leaned into Jason, careful not to put too much pressure on his injured torso. "Together, I like the sound of that."

Jason raised his glass to the sky. "To Ryman. To Theo. To Dan. To Tyrone. To Soloman. Rest peacefully."

"Rest peacefully," Marc said.

They both took a long, slow swallow.

Later, close to midnight, they lay naked beneath the covers. Jason was on his back, his head and shoulder propped on pillows. Marc was on his side, his fingers trailed through Jason's chest hair, circling his nipples. His skin was dark and mottled with bruises. Now Chantelle was behind bars, Jason would at last be able to heal, without further injury.

Sex had been a necessity. A life-affirming act in the face of so much death.

"What do you think will happen next?" Marc asked softly. "After today?"

"Do you mean for the city? It's got to get better. At least I hope it will. After the last two years, things can't get any worse. There's a lot of trust to be rebuilt. I'm not sure the police will ever repair the damage they've done."

"There was a strong sense of community tonight. All those people came together because they cared. It should count for something."

"Hmm. As long as lessons have been learned this time."

"And us?"

"Us?" Jason kissed the top of his head. "What would you like to happen with us?"

Marc slid his hand beneath the covers, placing his palm on the flat of Jason's abdomen. "I'd like some peace. Some quiet."

Jason let out a long sigh. "I'm all in for that."

"A chance for us to get to know each other better. Without the threat of murder or violence."

"Even better."

Marc smiled. They were on the same page, both of them wanting the same thing. Their relationship might have begun in the worst circumstances, but that didn't mean they couldn't change things for the better. They could even grow old together.

He was racing ahead.

Right now, they were safe and with each other.

After everything they had been through, it was the best place they could be.

Sign up for our newsletter and find out about all our romance book releases, eBook sales and promotions, sneak peeks and FREE romance books!

Want to see more from this author?
Here's a taster for you to enjoy!

Jagged Shores: North Point
Thom Collins

Excerpt

It was early evening in mid-July. A strong breeze came in from the east as Arnie Walker and AJ, his nine-year-old son, reached the top of the point. The sky was an unspoiled blue, but the wind whipped around them, pulling at their hair and clothes, and Arnie was glad he'd made the boy put on a hoodie before leaving their holiday home.

"You're not cold, are you?"

"No way," AJ replied, hurrying ahead.

"Stay away from the edge," Arnie warned.

North Point stood a hundred and six feet above the town of Nyemouth on the Northumberland coast, where the River Nye met the North Sea. From its peak they could see the entire town beneath them, nestled in the steep valley. The river ran through the center of the gorge, a broad curving waterway separating the two sides of the town. On the south bank, in a wide basin, was the marina, and just beyond, the green park and bandstand in the town square.

Ahead of them, to the east, was the vast, open vista of the North Sea. The strengthening wind created white tips on the waves of the incoming tide. Arnie gazed appreciatively at the view, filling his lungs with fresh, salty air. He'd missed this place. Coming here now, with his son, awoke memories of his own childhood, long-ago summers when he'd played on the point and the beach below, fishing in the rock pools at low tide or watching the yachts sail into the harbor. Some of the happiest, most innocent days of his life had been spent here.

"Dad, can we go down to the beach?" AJ asked.

Arnie saw some of that long-lost innocence in his son's face. He heard it in the pitch of his voice. "Not tonight. The tide is coming in. Besides, we'll be having dinner soon. Aren't you hungry?"

AJ stared at the rocks below and the sandy stretch of beach farther north. "The sea is miles out yet. Can't we go down for ten minutes? Five?"

"I'll take you to the beach tomorrow. I promise. The tide might look a long way out now, but it comes in fast. Really fast. The path to get down is a good mile ahead. By the time we get there, that beach will be gone. And we don't want to get stuck down on the rocks. The sea can come in and wash you away. It's dangerous."

AJ gazed longingly at the shore, unconvinced by his father's warning.

"Tomorrow," Arnie said firmly. "Remember, we've a whole five weeks ahead of us. That's plenty of time to play on the beach. When the summer is over, you'll be sick of picking sand out of your bum"

AJ giggled, thumping his hand playfully against his father's waist. "Sand doesn't get in your bum."

"Sand gets *everywhere*. In between your toes, in your ears, in your hair." He mussed AJ's short blond hair for effect.

The boy squealed with delight and squirmed away. "Stop it."

"Come on, we'll walk five more minutes before heading back. Are you hungry yet?"

"No."

"Well, I'm starving, so let's go."

They continued north along the cliff, keeping clear of the edge. Safety on the point had been something drilled into Arnie by his own parents from a young age, and it was a message he'd never forgotten. Like all coastal areas, the cliffs and rock faces here suffered from erosion and collapses. Harsh winters and rough seas took their toll.

When Arnie was AJ's age, the father of a boy from school had been killed on a beach outside of town when the cliff face collapsed. It was a vivid memory. Another summer, two people had died when they'd fallen over the edge and had been washed out to sea. A week later, one of the bodies had become tangled in the nets of a fishing boat. They had never recovered the second corpse. Despite the beauty here, there was immense danger. The natural elements had to be respected at all times.

Arnie had spent his life until the age of eighteen in Nyemouth, in the town below. He had moved to London to study drama and film editing but had never lost touch with the area. His parents were still here, in the house he grew up in. Though his career prevented him from coming back as often as he'd like to, a part of his heart remained.

Arnie Walker was thirty-four years old. He had dark blond hair, thick on top and conservatively short at the back and sides. His eyes were an intense, icy shade of blue. With an angular jaw and wide mouth, he was classically handsome. His six-foot-four frame and wholesome good looks were a striking combination. Arnie was a familiar one to TV audiences, having starred in several high-profile series, but despite a brief period of international success in his midtwenties, he could walk around without attracting too much attention. He'd never been the type to court publicity, avoiding the media throughout his career and preferring to focus on his work. Though they recognized him, most people respected his privacy, especially when he was with AJ.

That was especially true here in Nyemouth. It was a small community with a population of just over six thousand. Many of the long-time residents knew his family or remembered him as a kid. Arnie Walker was just a local boy who'd done well for himself. He'd never lost touch with where he came from. A Nyemouth boy, he was one of them, and people respected him for that.

"Dad, can we get a dog?"

An inevitable question, though Arnie hadn't expected to hear it so soon. They'd arrived yesterday and had spent two days catching up with family, including his sister and her black Labrador, Benji. AJ had fallen in love with the animal at first sight.

"We don't have time to look after a dog properly," Arnie said.

"We can make time."

"It's not that easy. I have to go to work. You have to go to school."

"I'll look after it. I'll get up extra early to take it for walks."

"And what will it do all day when we're not there? Dogs need to go out for the toilet. It's not fair to leave them locked up so long."

"It can stay in the garden when we're out."

"And in the winter? When it gets cold. Then what?"

"You can buy him a kennel."

Typical kid, Arnie thought. He had an answer for everything. He'd been exactly the same at that age. It had probably driven his parents crazy. "Let's see how the summer goes," he said. "You can play with Aunty Sophie's dog and take him for walks."

"Then we'll get our own dog when we go home?" AJ's eyes were wide and opportunistic.

"I didn't say that."

"But you'll think about it?"

"We'll see how it goes. That's all I'll say for now."

AJ grinned, on the face of it convinced his father had committed to buying him a puppy. "Can we have fish and chips for dinner tonight?"

Arnie laughed. "If that's what you want."

A female runner came up behind them, swerved out of their way and jogged ahead, an impressive sight in her pale blue sportswear. Arnie watched her admiringly. He'd promised himself a couple of lazy days off before getting back into a fitness routine. The cliffs along the point would make an attractive route as long as the weather held. If he came out of town, followed the walking trail, then looped back around, he would arrive where he'd started on the north bank of the river. It would be a five-, maybe six-mile trek. Not bad at all.

"I think we'll turn around in another minute," he told AJ. The wind was strengthening and the warmth of the sun had faded in the early evening.

"Can we go for fish and chips, then?"

Arnie nodded. "I said so, didn't I? Am I right in thinking you're hungry now?"

"Starving," AJ said.

Up ahead, the runner drew level with a small, bushy hollow. As she passed, a figure stepped out of the bushes. Dressed in a black hoodie and dark pants, they must have been hiding there. In an instant, Arnie knew something was not right.

The dark stranger rushed at the woman, came up behind her and threw both arms around her. The next moment, the figure lifted her off her feet and carried her toward the cliff edge.

"Oh my God." Arnie couldn't believe what was happening. They were around two hundred yards ahead of them. "Stay here," he shouted at AJ, running forward.

The woman struggled in the stranger's grip, but he held her tight. She kicked her legs helplessly against empty air and the sound of her scream was carried away on the wind. It seemed to happen with the heavy feel of a nightmare. Arnie's legs were leaden as he ran toward them, making painfully slow progress. *This can't be happening.*

The stranger was less than two feet away from the edge of the cliff. They swung the woman to one side, gaining momentum, and as they did, Arnie caught a glimpse beneath the hoodie. Their features were black and blank — a ski-mask or balaclava under the hood. The stranger bent at the knees, then swung, straightened up and threw the woman clear over the edge.

With a roar of despair, Arnie pressed forward.

The woman appeared to hang weightless in the air — a terrifying trick of the mind — before she plummeted from sight. The hooded figure didn't wait to admire their malicious handiwork. They were already running back in the direction they'd come from. Arnie raced for the spot where he'd last seen the woman.

Please let her be hanging on, just over the edge. He knew before he got there it was a hopeless thought.

"Dad," AJ yelled from somewhere behind.

He was about to tell him to stay back when he remembered the danger they were in. He looked around. No sign of the stranger, but it didn't mean the psycho had gone. Given the ease with which they'd thrown a grown woman over the cliff, a boy like AJ would take no effort. "Come here," he urged. "Stay close."

"What happened to the lady?" AJ asked.

"That's what Daddy needs to find out." Arnie glanced around again. The hollow from where the stranger had ambushed the woman was clear. There was no one else in sight. He pointed at the area. "AJ, I want you to keep looking that way. Do you hear me? Keep watching in that direction and if you see anyone coming — anyone — you shout at the top of your voice. Do you understand?"

Pale-faced and shaken, AJ nodded.

"Good lad," Arnie said, managing to sound far calmer than he felt. "Dad is going to see if he can help the lady, but remember, I want you to shout as loud as possible and let me know if anyone comes this way."

He nodded vigorously. "I will."

Arnie took a deep breath and approached the precipice. The grassy surface gave way to sandstone for the last few feet. Craning forward, he looked down. The tide came across the rocks below with some force, throwing up huge white plumes. He couldn't see her.

"Hello," he yelled, holding out hope she was clinging to the rock face below him. "Can you hear me?"

Nothing, just the crash of waves and the howl of wind. He put his foot right on the edge and leaned farther out. Now he could see more of the base. There she was. A tiny figure, a hundred and fifty feet below, in her blue and black Lycra. She lay face down, one arm beneath her, the other stretched to the side, about two meters from where the waves crashed against the rocks.

"Shit." It would not take long for the tide to reach her. He pulled his phone out of his pocket and dialed emergency.

"Which service do you require?" asked the operator.

"Coastguard," he said urgently. "A woman has gone over the cliff at North Point." He explained what had happened as calmly as he could and gave their exact position. "She's beneath me right now, but hurry. The tide is rising fast. She doesn't have long."

There was a lifeboat station in Nyemouth marina. Once a crew was assembled, it would only take the boat minutes to reach this spot, but raising a crew was a bigger concern. Like most lifeboat stations, Nyemouth was run by volunteers. Their pagers would already have gone off, but the boat, an Atlantic 85, required a crew of at least three before setting off. Depending on where they were when the pagers sounded, it could take ten minutes before the boat was ready to launch.

Looking at the incoming tide, Arnie wondered if the woman had that long. There was no way to reach her from here. The rock face was steep . A proficient climber with the right equipment could do it, but they would never get the woman back up that way. The only other route was the distant footpath down to the beach, but the section of rocks on which she lay would already be cut off by the tide.

The lifeboat was her only hope of survival. Provided they reached her in time.

Provided she was still alive.

"Dad," AJ called from behind. "Dad, is the lady okay?"

The boy was facing the other way. Arnie went to him. He trembled, frightened and cold. Arnie crouched and put his arms around him. "Don't worry. The lifeboat will soon be here. They'll look after her."

"Why did the man throw her off the cliff?"

He hugged AJ tighter. "I don't know, son. Try not to think about that. The man has gone now."

"He…he might come back."

"Sssh. It's all right. I won't let him hurt you."

They had witnessed a murder. An attempted murder at best. *Impossible.* It was what happened in TV shows and movies. In his own career, Arnie had played victims and murderers, but it was always fake. Even with detailed research, he'd never considered the reality of the crime. Until now. Watching a man—surely it had to be a man—pick up a woman and throw her over a huge precipice without hesitation.

A cold shudder ran through him.

It was an act of complete evil. Would AJ ever be the same after seeing that?

Arnie rose, stretching to look down into the Nye valley. Too far away to make out any activity in the marina. How long had it been since he'd made the call? Five minutes? Longer? Then he saw it. The gray and orange streak as the Atlantic 85 lifeboat shot out of the marina, leaving a wide wake as she headed for the mouth of the river and the open sea. *Thank God.*

Arnie told AJ to stay where he was while he went to look down again. The sea was lapping over the edge of the rocks, the spray washing over her body. His heart raced faster. She did not have long until the cold water claimed her. The lifeboat had turned left out of the river mouth and powered up the coast.

Would they even see her? How visible could a prone figure at the foot of a cliff be to anyone watching from the sea? He looked down again. She was so tiny. They'd be sure to miss her.

Arnie pulled out his phone and activated the flashlight. He was directly above the woman. He stood with the phone held high, the light directed toward the boat.

"Come on," he cried, desperately. "She's here. Right here."

"Dad," AJ called. "Is the lifeboat coming?"

It did not look like it. The boat cruised north, scanning the shore. They were going too far. Arnie stretched higher, waving his phone frantically.

"Over here." AJ, right behind him, waved his arms and shouted. "Here."

"Don't come too close," Arnie warned him.

"But they're going the wrong way."

Then, at sea, the boat turned and headed directly toward them.

"They've seen us," he told AJ with relief. "It's all right, they've seen us."

They fixed the boat on the spot where the woman lay. With the treacherous rocks and back flow from the waves, getting to her would not be easy. The Atlantic 85 was built for maneuverability, but even that would struggle in these circumstances.

Arnie prayed they were not too late.

About the Author

Thom Collins is the author of *Closer by Morning*, with Pride Publishing. His love of page turning thrillers began at an early age when his mother caught him reading the latest Jackie Collins book and promptly confiscated it, sparking a life-long love of raunchy novels.

Thom has lived in the North East of England his whole life. He grew up in Northumberland and now lives in County Durham with his husband and two cats. He loves all kinds of genre fiction, especially bonkbusters, thrillers, romance and horror. He is also a cookery book addict with far too many titles cluttering his shelves. When not writing he can be found in the kitchen trying out new recipes. He's a keen traveler but with a fear of flying that gets worse with age, but since taking his first cruise in 2013 he realized that sailing is the way to go.

Thom loves to hear from readers. You can find his contact information, website details and author profile page at https://www.firstforromance.com

ENTWINED PUBLISHING